Drawn to Him

Tammy Mannersly

Drawn to Him
Copyright © 2020 Tammy Mannersly
All rights reserved.

ISBN: (ebook) 978-1-949931-77-8
(print) 978-1-949931-78-5

Inkspell Publishing
207 Moonglow Circle #101
Murrells Inlet, SC 29576

Edited By Yezanira Yenecia
Cover art By Najla Qamber

CHAPTER 1

The tiny bell on the front door of the store tinkled portentously in the quiet calm of the room as it announced the arrival of a new customer. Finishing the careful stroke on the canvas in front of her, Erica Townsend turned to her small, mostly-elderly class.

"Using the same brush, continue your vertical strokes, adding more tree trunks to our scene." She motioned to the enlarged photograph of a sylvan landscape, which was clipped atop her own wooden easel.

As several of her students nodded, Erica pointed to a rotund gentleman with a tartan beret in the back row. "No need to go overboard, Hamish. Less is more at times, remember?"

He touched the tip of his hat in salute, while the others continued in their work.

Beside him, a ginger-haired woman wearing a blotchy smock pointed her paintbrush in Erica's direction. "I'll keep an eye on him for you, sweetheart."

"Thanks, Jocelyn."

Winking at the older woman, Erica climbed to her feet

and rounded the wall of open shelves separating her store, Unique Art Boutique, into two individual spaces. Leaving the classroom behind, she entered the gallery and purchasable art supplies part of the shop. It still gave her a warm feeling, seeing her dream fulfilled. She had wanted to establish a place where her passion for art—creating it, teaching it, displaying it—could be enjoyed and shared by all. Then five years ago, needing to escape Brisbane after her mother's passing and another failed relationship, she'd come to the idyllic little town of Montville in the Sunshine Coast Hinterland in Queensland, and done just that.

Erica smoothed her hands over her white apron, now mottled with different hues of dried paint, hoping to remove the residue of green goop on her fingers before it ended up on her denim shorts or gray tank top. She didn't have many clothes left which weren't in some way stained by her profession.

Approaching her customer from behind, taking in the baby pink dress draped over the feminine figure, Erica smiled. "Can I help you?"

"Yes." The young woman turned, her familiar emerald eyes brightening. Her delicate features and light-blonde pixie-cut made her look even younger than her twenty-something years. "I need a canvas and some acrylics."

Moving behind the counter to the rack of small paint tubes against the wall, Erica gestured to her wares. "What size were you after? I have the acrylics in two ounces all the way up to sixty-four"—her hand waved toward the shelving on her left—"and the canvases come in square, rectangular—our smallest being the four-by-four inch. I think the biggest I have left in-store is a thirty-six-by-forty-eight, but I can always order in larger, even smaller if you'd prefer."

"Do you have the biggest canvas nearby? I'd like to check it over first, see if it's big enough."

Erica nodded. "In the storeroom, out the back." She looked closely at the young woman, noting a familiarity.

"You work down the road, don't you? At Forrest's Organics, the fresh produce store? It's … Lauren, isn't it?"

The blonde woman grinned. "Yes, Lauren Perry. We've crossed paths a couple of times. You used to come into the store all the time a few years back."

"Yeah. When I first came to town, I started on a fitness kick. I was only buying organic, eating fruit and veggies, trying to keep up with the local health fanatics. It didn't last long though. I couldn't live without pizza and chocolate … or wine. Out of everything from back then, yoga is the only thing I've stuck to."

Lauren's eyes lit up. "Did you know we have organic chocolate and wine in-store? Even organic, nonalcoholic wine."

"Trying to save me from the dark side, are you?" Erica chuckled.

As she shrugged, Lauren's smile remained sweet and kind.

With another laugh, Erica motioned for Lauren to wait. "I'll be back in a moment with the canvas."

She headed for an open doorway to her right, flicking on a light switch inside the narrow room as she entered. Labeled brown cardboard boxes were stacked against the wall nearest the entrance, while tall, static shelving, full of inventory, hugged the parallel walls, tapering the room even tighter. At the very back, plastic-wrapped canvases of varying sizes rested alongside each other. Reaching them, Erica dug around, propping some aside to get access to the bigger ones.

Distracted by thoughts of her class, of completing the landscape painting, Erica moved a little faster. Once she'd made enough space to retrieve the largest canvas, she grabbed the thick frame and hauled the huge item up and out from the wall. Careful to clear the others she'd stacked beside it, she spun around but connected with the shelving structure to her right. Although it was bolted to the floor, it shook slightly, and she heard a couple of large *thuds* against the wooden floorboards.

She growled her displeasure and mentally scolded herself for attempting to move the gigantic item, instead of just taking Lauren into the storeroom to inspect it.

Sighing, Erica lowered the monstrosity to get a better look at the obstructions in front of her. She'd recently received an order of gesso—a white mixture used to prime the canvas before painting—and had restocked the shelf until the front two tubs sat slightly over the edge. Now those round containers were on the floor beyond her left foot—one on its side and one on its lid.

At least nothing breakable had fallen. Lifting the huge canvas higher again and holding it to her right, Erica stepped over the first obstacle. When she lifted her left foot over the second, the sound of footsteps entering the room had her gaze drifting upward.

Lauren let out a high-pitched squeak. "Are you okay?"

Erica nodded as her foot came down and clipped the edge of the circular tub. The container rolled, taking her heel with it, and she raised the canvas in the air struggling for balance. A garbled sound—part squeal, part yip—left her lips as she hit the floor hard on her right knee. Her bare skin skidded along the coarse wooden floorboards as her foot continued its ride. A split-second passed, something Erica experienced in slow-motion, and the tub popped free of her ankle before skittering across to the doorway. In her desperation for stability, she lowered the canvas and smacked herself in the face. When the ordeal was finally over, she was stretched across the floor, one leg in front, one behind, feeling sore, stupid, and sorry for herself, but so grateful her love of yoga had saved her from pulling a hamstring or breaking bone.

"Oh my God!" Lauren ran over to her. "Did I do that?"

Lowering the canvas to the floor, Erica rested it alongside the static shelves beside her. She brushed a loose lock of dark hair from her eyes before taking Lauren's outstretched hand.

"No. No." Erica shook her head, feeling everything ache as she stood. "Just me. My bad luck, really. I can be clumsy."

The *thudding* of more footsteps drew her attention to the storeroom's entry as she released Lauren's hand and brushed her own on her apron.

"What's happened?" Jocelyn's announcement was audible before she'd even entered.

When she came into view, her freckled cheeks were pinker than usual and her curly red-hair was gathering a frizz from her briskness. Erica smiled at her reassuringly as she adjusted the chocolate-brown bun atop her own head.

"Nothing to see here, Jocelyn. I had a little trip but survived the journey." She gestured at the large canvas, which was now sporting a slight indentation from where her nose had bashed into it. "Not sure I can say the same thing about the canvas."

"Oh, it's fine," Lauren said quickly, waving Erica's comment away with a flick of her wrist. "It's perfect. I'll take it."

Erica frowned. "It's damaged stock now. I can order in another."

Lauren shook her head. "It'll do, really."

As Erica opened her mouth to argue the point further, Jocelyn interrupted.

"Ladies!" It was almost a shriek.

"What?" Erica noticed the horror in the older woman's eyes and followed the direction of Jocelyn's outstretched index finger.

It was aimed at Erica's knee, the one that had dragged along the rough floorboards as she'd skidded ungracefully into the splits. There had been a slight stinging sensation, a constant ache, but Erica hadn't realized the damage she'd inflicted upon herself until now. Dark, garnet-red blood was thick in the grooves of the mutilated skin, while congealed snail-trails of scarlet crept down her shin.

Although the pain was distracting, she noticed it was only a flesh wound and bound to be a minor one once she'd had the time to clean it up.

"Oh dear." Lauren gasped.

"I'll call an ambulance." The concern in Jocelyn's tone was enough to have both of the younger women looking up at her again.

"No, Jocelyn—" Erica reached out in an effort to stop her, but the ginger-haired woman had already retreated inside the main room of the shop.

Fighting back the urge to limp, Erica hurried after her. She found her at the display counter, the cordless phone to her ear.

"Put the phone down." It was an order, said with only the slightest hint of menace.

Just the thought of having to explain herself to a pair of highly-skilled paramedics if Jocelyn was successful, was enough to have dread sitting heavily in Erica's stomach. She could already imagine their looks of displeasure.

Yes, sir. … It's just a skinned knee, sir. … Yes, I understand what an emergency is. … Yes, I know I'm taking your services away from someone who really needs your help, but you see, my friend here, she called you.

"Jocelyn." She offered her another warning.

"Don't use that tone with me, Erica."

She lifted her own dark eyebrow in challenge. "I am not going to the hospital over a scraped knee."

Jocelyn's eyes narrowed. "You're such a stubborn young woman."

Erica took that as a compliment, but then noticed the older woman's expression change, her gaze flickering across the shop as though concentrating on something only she was privy to.

"Yes. We need an ambulance."

Erica tried to snatch the phone away from Jocelyn's ear. "No, we don't."

"What's going on in here?" A male voice interrupted

the jostle of hands.

Both of them glanced along the wall of open shelving, noticing the interest from those still seated in the classroom on the other side, before seeing Hamish striding over to them, his usually jolly countenance now full of concern.

Erica looked back at Jocelyn, giving her an opportunity to explain, but as the milliseconds passed, the attractive older woman's gray-green eyes became even more defiant.

Erica placed her hands on her hips. "Okay, what do you want?"

Jocelyn grinned smugly and covered the mouthpiece. "You don't want an ambulance, don't want to go to the hospital, fine. Then you let me take you to the doctor. I know what you're like, Erica. You'll patch this up yourself and wait for it to get infected before you even consider going to see a professional."

"I will n—" Erica would have finished her retort had Jocelyn not removed her hand from the bottom of the phone and dared her to continue with that twinkle in her eye. "Fine." It was said through gritted teeth. "I'll go to the doctor. Now, hang up and let them help someone who needs it."

"Sorry," Jocelyn spoke into the mouthpiece. "False alarm." A button *beeped* as she ended the call. Placing the telephone back in its cradle, she turned to Erica. "All right, let's go."

Erica raised her hands stopping Jocelyn's forward momentum. "We're not going right now?"

Jocelyn frowned and reached again for the phone.

"Okay, okay. We're going *now*."

Erica looked over at Hamish, who was stroking his chin thoughtfully, then at Lauren, who had carried the gigantic canvas out of the storeroom without falling over like a klutz, and finally across to her dedicated class of elderly citizens, who were trying so hard to appear as though their concentration had returned to their work.

"What am I going to do about the shop?" Erica gestured toward the classroom. "The lesson?"

"Hamish will take care of the store while we're gone, won't you, Hamish?"

Hamish was obviously startled by Jocelyn's announcement but didn't argue with her.

He nodded. "Whatever you need, Erica."

She gave him an appreciative smile as Jocelyn continued.

"He can serve this young lady"—she waved a hand toward Lauren—"and we can reschedule our lesson for another time." Jocelyn peered through the open shelves at the people on the other side. "Isn't that right, everyone?"

Unanimous nodding and a few muffled whispers seemed to be all Jocelyn needed in response. She grabbed Erica's hand and led her out from behind the counter.

"I'm so sorry, guys." Erica's voice was a pitch higher than usual as she addressed those in the class. "I'll give you all a call later to see if there's another day this week that will suit everyone."

Passing Lauren, Erica offered her a helpless look of apology, before being dragged closer to Hamish. There, Jocelyn released her while she ducked into the classroom to retrieve her handbag.

Once Jocelyn was behind him, Hamish's concerned expression flashed to humor. He tilted his head in the older woman's direction, and his eyes widened, then rolled.

Erica stifled a hoot of laughter with a cough. "Hamish, could you please give Lauren a discount on the canvas when you ring it up?" She noticed Lauren raise a hand as if to dispute, but refused to give her the opportunity. "Don't let her talk you out of it. The canvas is damaged, and she deserves it, having put up with all of this." Erica motioned around the room, to the canvas, her knee, and then pointed a thumb at Jocelyn who had re-entered behind Hamish.

"Oi," the older woman quipped. "You should be

thanking me. I'm just looking out for you, missy."

There were a few playful thank yous from the other room, which swiftly became giggles.

"Come on, my girl." Jocelyn snatched up her hand. "Let's go tackle your fear of doctors."

TAMMY MANNERSLY

CHAPTER 2

An ancient wrinkled woman—with more hair on her top lip than on her eyebrows—pointed once again at the pus-filled hole in her lower jaw where one of the last of her few teeth had previously resided. The portly middle-aged man with thick black hair sitting beside her wrapped an arm around her shoulders.

"No, Mama. I told you before. He is a doctor, not a dentist."

Matt Garrick offered his patients a warm smile from where he sat across the desk in his cozy, brightly-lit office. Tearing another completed prescription from his pad, he fought the urge to peek at his wristwatch a third time.

"Mr. Agnelli, Mother Agnelli, is there anything further I can personally help you with besides, say ... a referral to a good dental clinic?"

Mr. Agnelli shook his head. "Thank you, Dr. Garrick. That's very generous, but we already have a family dentist. The renewed prescriptions should be all for today."

As Matt handed him the final piece of paper, Mr. Agnelli nodded a non-verbal thanks before helping his elderly mother to her feet. She muttered something in Italian and slapped at his hand. He smiled sheepishly at

Matt, who had come around his desk, manila folder in one hand, to open the door for them.

"Until next time then," Matt told him, "take care of yourself." He bent lower to address the wizened, white-haired woman already exiting the room. "You too, Mother Agnelli."

She waved a hand at Matt, dismissing him, and then shuffled into the quiet waiting room. Matt followed them out, slipping his free hand around the fabric of his white coat and into the side pocket of his black slacks. He watched them quarrel mildly in Italian, attracting the attention of a modest, middle-aged couple seated beside the reception desk. On the other side of the counter, Melina grinned up at the Agnellis, deep smile lines creasing her face while her brown eyes sparkled behind her horn-rimmed glasses. She noticed Matt looking their way and gave him that sweet, motherly wink he was becoming accustomed to.

"Matt."

The hushed masculine voice had him glancing across the corridor toward the second and only other office in the small house turned family practice. Even though the entire premises had been refurbished, it still held the intimacy and quaintness of the old turn-of-the-century building.

Doctor Nathan Lewis stepped next to him, his white coat swaying over his designer checkered shirt and navy trousers as he thrust his expensive smartphone in front of Matt's face.

"Speed-dating is on again tonight in the town hall. Are you keen for a round two?"

Matt raised his eyes from the screen, away from details of the event and the persuasive photo of an attractive couple kissing, to stare at the slightly taller, rangier man. "I'm starting to think you need to find a new wingman, Nate."

"What?" He yanked the phone back. "Last week wasn't a total flop."

Matt frowned at his longtime friend, the man who had become a buddy back in college over twelve years ago and who had recently talked him into becoming a partner in his practice in the peaceful country town of Montville. When he'd agreed to the change, having needed it after tiring of the pressure, the people, and the busy lifestyle in Brisbane city, Matt hadn't realized getting back out into the dating scene would be part of the deal.

"For you maybe," Matt quipped as he headed over to the reception desk, "but within the absolute whirlwind of single women that flew by that night, I had two marriage proposals, an offer to take part in creating a brood of eleven, and one woman who just stared at me for our full two minutes."

Following him, Nate shrugged. "Being part of a small community means you get lumped with the lot, castoffs and all. You've got to sift through them to find the gold."

"You go dig for your treasure then." Matt placed the Agnelli's file into his out-tray, glancing at his empty in-tray, before looking back at Nate. "But, I'll wait until you find an alternative to speed-dating before I click back into wingman mode."

Melina chuckled, her platinum-blonde bob swaying with her movement, as she gave Mr. Agnelli his receipt.

Grimacing, Nate scratched at his neat auburn beard, his angular features giving him the appearance of a handsome movie villain. "What else is there? I'm not ready to try it online."

Mr. Agnelli risked a look in their direction and leaned a little closer, ensuring his arm still remained securely around his mother's shoulders. "You can try the local bushwalking group," he suggested shyly. "Or Unique Art Boutique on Main Street offers nighttime life drawing classes." His bold features brightened. "That's where I met my Cathy. We've been together three years this June."

Mother Agnelli mumbled something, which sounded rather scathing in Italian, and Mr. Agnelli returned to her, ushering her toward the front door as he waved a friendly good-bye.

Matt watched Nate, noticing his interest in the older gentleman's ideas as Melina gave them her full attention.

"I've heard good things about that place, too. My Samuel's there now for his regular Tuesday acrylics course." Seeing she'd gotten their interest, Melina smiled slyly. "But, you know, if you'd really like to meet a *nice* girl, I know plenty of available young ladies."

Nate snatched the top file from his own in-tray. "Not another set-up, Melina. The last one barely said a word to me the entire night."

Melina scowled at him. "She was a nice church girl. Besides, I didn't mean for you, Mr. Eternal Bachelor. I was talking to Matthew." She gave Matt a wide, encouraging grin.

Nate rolled his eyes.

As he freed his hand from his trouser pocket to run it through his thick, dark hair, Matt cleared his throat. "I'll have to think about it, Melina, but thank you."

When Melina opened her mouth to continue, the front door burst open drawing everyone's attention.

"We need to see a doctor," a mature, ginger-haired woman announced enthusiastically as she entered the waiting room dragging a long-legged beauty into the room behind her.

"There's no urgency," added the exotic young woman, her attractive coffee-brown eyes shooting a fierce glare at the redhead.

"Jocelyn?" Melina stood, hurrying around the counter to greet the older woman as Nate and Matt inched closer to the action. "What's happened? Are you okay?"

"It's not me, it's Erica." Jocelyn pulled the shapely brunette forward in front of all of them.

The young woman—Erica—gazed up at Nate, a light blush coloring her cheeks mixing exquisitely with the mocha undertones of her skin as she swept a chocolate lock of hair from her eyes.

"I'm fine, really," her sweet voice reassured them. "It's just my knee. I had a little fall."

All eyes dropped to her long, slender legs. At the sight of her right knee, all torn flesh and congealed garnet, Matt took a step forward, eager to help.

"You're Erica, Erica Townsend, right?" Nate stuck out a hand.

As the gorgeous creature shook it appreciatively, offering his friend the goddamn-sexiest smile he'd ever seen, Matt mentally cursed his best buddy. Nate had always been quicker on the draw when it came to beautiful women.

"You own Unique Art Boutique?" Nate didn't wait for her answer. "That's so funny. We were just talking about you. About your shop."

"Only good things, I hope."

"They're looking for somewhere to meet nice girls," Melina informed Jocelyn, earning her a glare from Nate. "Mr. Agnelli told them about the life drawing class."

"Oh." Erica was surprised but quickly recovered. "I was serving a nice girl earlier this morning. I'm not sure if she'll be there on life drawing night, but I know plenty of other single ladies who often attend."

As Matt watched, Nate upped his charisma, attempting to hide his obvious discomfort with a confident-sounding chuckle. "If they're anything like you, Erica, we'll find ourselves lucky to be in the same room with them."

"You always thought you were a charmer, Nathan," taunted Jocelyn. "Now, if you wouldn't mind taking care of the patient."

She pushed Erica closer to him, making something heavy drop into the bottom of Matt's stomach.

How was Nate always the chosen one?

"Sorry, Jocelyn, but Dr. Lewis has another patient." Melina gestured to the mature couple seated beside the counter, keenly observing the whole interaction.

The woman offered them a satisfied nod before straightening her perfectly starched, pale yellow dress, while her husband's nose rose higher.

Nate opened his mouth as if to protest, but Melina waved a hand in his face and grabbed Erica by the arm, dragging her in front of Matt.

"Dr. Garrick is free. He will take good care of you."

Again, the stunning brunette blushed.

"Dr. Garrick, I presume?" She smiled that sexy grin at him, gripping his heart and igniting his blood.

Didn't anyone else notice the sensuality of that look, the raw heat behind it, or was it just him?

Trying to keep the appearance of professionalism, Matt raised a hand and motioned in the direction of his office. "Shall we go get you cleaned up?"

When she moved away, following his silent instruction, she left an intoxicating scent in her wake. Strawberries and vanilla. Matt almost groaned. Was there nothing about this woman that wasn't perfect?

Jocelyn and Melina began chatting quietly as Matt followed Erica, meeting Nate's eyes as he passed. Although undoubtedly disappointed by the missed opportunity, Nate's secretive thumbs-up of encouragement said enough. If he couldn't get to know this ravishing beauty himself, then he considered Matt the next best man.

CHAPTER 3

Closing the door to his office had never felt so final, never given him such a feeling of intimacy as it did now. Matt was all alone with the most alluring woman he had ever met. No matter how macho he liked to pretend he was, how suave he tried to remind himself he could be, nerves were still getting the best of him.

"Do you want me on the table?"

Matt spun around, his voice catching in his throat. "Pardon?"

"Is it easier for you to check my knee if I sit on the examination table?"

He released a deep breath. "Good idea. Yes, thank you."

Erica gave him a quizzical look but went to the back of the room.

As her hips swayed, Matt caught himself staring at her ass, then quickly forced his gaze upward when she turned around. He continued to watch while she did a little jump to position herself on the table, admiring how her generous bust jiggled with the movement.

God, he was going to Hell.

Matt swallowed. "So, what brought you here today?"

She tilted her head as she stroked a loose strand of hair behind her ear again.

He coughed. "I mean, how did you hurt yourself?"

"Oh." Erica glanced down at her knee, stretching the tanned skin around it as though trying to get a better look at the damage. "A really big canvas knew my weakness."

Matt opened the cabinet opposite his desk to retrieve a packet of alcohol-free wipes and a bottle of saline solution. "And what's that?"

"I'm a bit of a klutz."

He chuckled, closing the cabinet before snatching a new pair of sterile green gloves from the box on his desk. "Is that so? Do I need to handcuff you to the table so you don't fall off?"

Erica smirked at him and something sparkled in her fascinating eyes.

Matt froze, his breath caught sharply.

Shit. He'd said *handcuff*, he'd meant to say strap. Geez, that wasn't much better. Talk about Freudian slip.

He cleared his throat and continued over to her. "Sorry. Terrible joke."

Her grin widened and she chuckled at him. "I thought I was supposed to be the nervous one. I'm the one who's afraid of doctors."

As he lowered the items to the thin, sheet-covered mattress, Matt stiffened. He'd given himself away. What an idiot. It was nerves one, suaveness zero. Then something Erica had said resounded in his mind.

His eyes widened. "You're afraid of doctors?"

She shrugged as he moved his office chair in front of her. "You're the bearers of bad news. You poke and prod people with nasty instruments … and I'm afraid of needles."

Matt nodded in understanding and took a seat. "Ah, the needle thing." He slipped on the green surgical gloves. "You're not alone in that fear. I know a few big, manly men who faint at the sight of them." He pulled an alcohol-free wipe out of its packet. "Luckily, this shouldn't require anything so serious."

When he moved to touch the wipe to her skin, he noticed her hands clenching around the mattress on either side of her slender thighs. Pausing, he looked up at her.

Propped on the examination bed as she was, she sat substantially higher than him. Though Matt was tall enough, six-foot-one on a good day, Erica was only slightly shorter, which presented a different stance than the other patients he'd had in a similar position. His eye-level was dangerously close to her breasts, and gazing up along the supple line of her neck didn't help much either.

Would it be so wrong of him to wrap his hands around her waist and drag her down to his lap? To feel the softness of her curves against his body? To kiss her until the only pain she felt was the ardent hunger, the suffocating desire to screw his brains out?

A giant *yes* like a thunderclap from God echoed inside his head. *Yes, it's wrong.*

He looked up into her beautiful eyes, suddenly noticing the concern in them. "It will be okay," he reassured her.

"It's going to hurt, isn't it?" She winced.

The corners of his lips quirked upward. "Don't tell me—you're scared of pain, as well?"

Erica nibbled at her bottom lip, unconsciously enticing him, making him wish he could nibble it for her.

"I'm not a huge chicken," she began. "I can handle most things, but the stinging of an open wound, especially having it cleaned, is not one of my favorite pastimes."

"Luckily the wound doesn't look too serious, so I'll try to make it as painless as possible."

"I'd appreciate that." She stared at him, her gaze drifting down deep into his, the gleam in her eyes making his heart somersault.

He noticed her inhale deeply and hold it as he tried again, touching the wipe to her broken skin. When it connected, her breath hissed out, but then she calmed, her

21

limbs relaxing as he continued.

"See, you're tougher than you give yourself credit for." Matt added saline solution to the cloth to make it a little easier to clean the wound.

"It still hurts, but I'll do my best not to cry *bloody murder.*"

He laughed. When his eyes met hers, nerves got the better of him, and he was suddenly at a loss of what more to say. Swallowing, he stood and headed back over to the cabinet.

"Um …" *Damn it!* He felt his face flush with heat. He'd had to make it even more obvious that he was feeling like an anxious teenager. "So, the life drawing classes?" He gathered his courage and glanced up at her as he grabbed a pair of scissors, some gauze, and a roll of sticky bandage off the shelf. "Would you recommend them?" Matt wanted to slap himself in the forehead. *What a ridiculous question!* "For us, I mean. Nate and I. Sorry, Dr. Lewis and me."

He fought the urge to leave the room before he made even more of a fool of himself, and instead, headed back over to her. Erica was just smiling at him, that devilishly sultry grin that made him wish they were both naked.

"To meet women?" Her eyes glimmered curiously.

Matt did his best to hide the audible gulp as he swallowed once more and took a seat in front of her. "Yes. I guess." He shook his head. "It's more Nate's thing. He's looking for *the one*, you know, and I'm his wingman."

"So, you're just along for the ride?"

He cleared his throat as he measured out the gauze. "Pretty much."

"You're not keen to find your Miss Right then?"

Her teasing tone enticed Matt's gaze upward, and he found himself stuck, captured by her mesmerizing eyes.

"We do have some lovely young ladies who attend. Some of them even pose for the class. Are you sure I can't tempt you?"

Matt was frozen, he knew he was and couldn't help it. His hands were still poised holding the gauze above Erica's injured knee, and all he could do was stare at her.

Her words rang in his ears. *Are you sure I can't tempt you?*

Was she flirting with him? God, he hoped so.

She giggled. "Sorry. I didn't mean to scare you."

"No." Matt shook his head, unfreezing the rest of his body with that one movement. "No, you didn't."

"Good. I was worried I'd terrified you into a lifetime of bachelorhood."

He forced a smile. What would she say if she knew he'd felt the opposite, that maybe he didn't want to meet all those other women, because maybe she could be his *one*?

She'd probably say he was an idiot, which he probably was. He'd never even believed in love at first sight, had been pretty certain it was all a fairytale—but now? Lord, he was screwed.

"You're not ready then? Not ready to settle down?" Erica watched as Matt fiddled with the materials in his lap.

How could he answer that? *I wasn't ready fifteen minutes ago, but then I met you, and now I just might be.* Yeah, that would go down well. What in the world was wrong with him?

Using the scissors, Matt snipped the gauze down to size before resting it over the damp wound, using sticky bandage to secure it.

"Sorry, I'm not usually so nosy."

He looked up at her, but she was still watching his hands, his thumbs smoothing the bandage over her skin. "It's okay. Really."

Her brown eyes met his. "Thanks. I guess I hoped you might be a kindred spirit. Someone else who wasn't so caught up in the hype of true love, searching for a partner, the perfect marriage to complete them. I've dated my fair share of toads and never once did I stumble across a Prince Charming. That's sort of why I came here. I decided to choose my passion over—" She giggled. "Well,

23

another kind of *passion*."

The warmness of her smile had him mirroring it. "Sounds like we've had a similar experience in the dating pool. Only my toadettes weren't the main reason I left Brisbane behind. I needed a change of scenery, a change of pace, and when Nate called me about this opportunity a couple of months back, well, I couldn't turn it down."

"You didn't get a chance to read the fine print though, right?" She grinned at him, making his insides swirl. "Wingman wanted."

"Yeah. I missed that."

"It doesn't mean you can't enjoy yourself though. Come to the life drawing class. I promise I won't introduce you to anyone if you don't want me to, but I think I'd kind of like your company. Especially if Dr. Lewis decides to try to turn my class into the next big dating scene."

"I'd love to." His heart swelled.

Had she just asked him out? Maybe not in so many words, but surely this invitation was the next best thing.

Surprise widened her eyes for an instant. "Great. Our next class is at seven o'clock on Friday night."

With his heart now beating out a bongo rhythm, Matt took a calming breath. He gazed down at the neat dressing he'd finished applying to her injury and cleared his throat. "You're all good to go."

"Really?" She glanced down at her knee. "Well, that was more painless than I expected."

"See, not all of us doctors are terrifying."

"Not all doctors are like you, Dr. Garrick."

His cheeks heated, and, as he realized he was blushing, Matt became even more embarrassed. "You should probably call me, Matt."

Her expression warmed.

"Since we're going to be spending more time together, you know," he explained unnecessarily.

"Of course. Well," she drew out the word as she pushed herself off the examination table and onto her feet in front of him. "Until Friday then, Matt."

It took a moment for him to shake the incredible daydream that held him captivated. As she'd moved to stand, he'd hoped—God, he'd even prayed—she might just have fulfilled his fantasy—her smooth, long legs wrapping over him, straddling him as her lips found his.

Matt stood up abruptly, putting himself uncomfortably—or rather too comfortably—close to Erica. When their eyes met, his lips twisted in a nervous smile. Her pupils widened, and she breathed deeply, her ample chest thrusting out to meet his.

Matt knew he should move. His body tingled with the need to fight off this awkwardness, to either pull her into his arms and embrace her, or get out of the damn way. But, as usual, he froze.

Another inhale brought her even closer, her lips one final breath away. His skin prickled with a sensual electricity as he struggled to make the right decision. Should he take the risk or back away and hope for another opportunity? Was she caught by the same force he was, the same sexual attraction, an instinctive chemistry? Or were his delusions melding into reality?

Then it happened, that final breath, her lips snuck closer, brushing his, leaving a scalding spark, a blistering burn where they'd briefly, barely touched his skin—and then they were gone.

Matt wasn't exactly sure *when* he'd closed his eyes, but when he opened them again Erica had disappeared.

The *click* of the door handle had him turning around. She was halfway out of his office before she turned back to look at him, to give him that deadly sexy smile, making his insides smolder and ache with a want he'd never experienced before.

A torrent of thoughts whirled through his head, driven to swirl faster with the knowledge that in these final few seconds, his last words needed to leave an impression, a very good impression.

"Make sure to keep it clean."

Erica's gorgeous eyes glittered back at him, and then she was gone, heading back into the waiting room to see Melina and Jocelyn.

Make sure to keep it clean?

Matt could have died right then and there. He could have said anything, anything at all. He could have said he hoped she had a nice day. He could have mentioned he'd see her at the art class on Friday. Even the corniest *"That was nice"* would have been a better option. But, no, the doctor voice in his head had won out and his concern over wound care had been the final impression his suave self had been willing to make. No *"Thanks for the kiss, you beautiful babe,"* just *"Make sure you don't get dirt on your injured knee."*

He slapped his hand over his face and closed his eyes.

CHAPTER 4

"Crap." It was a hushed word said as Erica took a bite of her ham and salad sandwich.

"Are you judging the quality of your food-making skills, or was that in reference to our conversation?"

Erica chewed her mouthful as she glared at Seeley Cabot, her good friend of five years. Seeley nipped off the end of a carrot stick with her teeth.

"Clearly I'm missing something." She spoke around the orange-colored chunks in her mouth. "Either you're not finding my storytelling of the goings on at the Montville Tavern all that interesting anymore, or there's something else up. If I had to place a bet, I'd put my money on it having something to do with that knee."

Seeley pointed at the creased bandage on her friend's right leg. Erica sighed in obvious acquiescence and stared at Seeley, taking in her asymmetrical caramel bob, keen blue eyes, and smug grin.

"Out with it." Seeley waved a fresh carrot stick at her demandingly.

"I did something bad today." Erica lowered her gaze to her half-eaten sandwich.

"Okay." Seeley nodded, pondering options as she took

in the picturesque greenery of the Russell Family Park around them. "You ... poked someone in the eye with a paintbrush?"

"No. How does that even relate to my knee?"

Seeley shrugged. "They could have kicked you in retaliation."

Erica shook her head. "No."

"Fine." Seeley relaxed her long bean-pole of a body back into the wooden park bench, revealing her lean belly between her cropped black tank and snug denim jeans. "You ... made a pass at Hamish, so Jocelyn threw her easel at you?"

A chuckle escaped Erica's lips, causing her grim expression to brighten. "No."

"Okay, I give up." Seeley raised her hands, the carrot stick balanced like a cigarette between her fingers. "You'll just have to tell me."

Erica watched the young children playing with their parents in the colorful, bark-floored playground in front of them. A little blonde girl in a sky-blue princess dress stood giggling at the peak of the short slippery-slide as her father waited at the bottom, trying to encourage her to take the plunge by waving a tatty teddy bear at her.

"You know how I told you when we first met that I'd decided to take a break from men, a break from dating to focus on my career?" Erica's gaze remained fixed on the little girl as she spoke.

"Yeah." Seeley nodded. "Five long years ago, and in that time I've tried to set you up on numerous occasions in an effort to snap you out of your self-imposed ban. I know for a fact it worked a couple of times."

The little girl's father let out a cheer as she pushed herself free from the top of the slide and slid down into his arms. A smile tugged at Erica's lips as she returned her attention to her friend.

"A couple of nights," she corrected. "There was no dating, no relationships. Just urges being fulfilled."

"Urges," Seeley snorted in amusement and bit off the end of the carrot stick she'd been fiddling with.

"Yes. Anyway …" Erica rolled her eyes, "I may be rethinking it." She lifted her hand, her thumb and index finger pinching close together but leaving the smallest of space in-between. "A tiny bit."

"Hallelujah!" Seeley gazed heavenward, lifting her hands in the same direction and then stopped, her eyes flicking back to Erica. "Who's the guy who's inspired this epiphany then?"

"What makes you think I'm going to tell you?"

"You will," Seeley said confidently. "So, this thing you *did* today, wasn't a *something* at all, but a *him*?"

"I didn't *do* any *hims*," Erica snapped as the man from the playground walked past them, his daughter's hand in his.

Seeley met his gaze. "Just practicing for the church choir," she told him, her tone surprisingly convincing.

His gaze narrowed with curiosity, but he smiled as he led his daughter toward their red sedan in the parking lot.

"I hate you," Erica growled.

Seeley only shrugged. "Can you at least tell me the specifics then if there was no actual *doing*?"

Erica placed her half-eaten sandwich in her plastic lunchbox. It was odd, there was an uneasiness in her stomach, a sort of hunger, but food was making her feel nauseated. It reminded her of the excitement she used to feel as a child before going on holidays, mixed with that sinking dread that came with the fear of missing out, the worry that the things you were looking forward to, the things you wanted desperately, might never eventuate.

"I sort of kissed him."

Seeley's eyes widened. "Your mystery man?"

Erica shook herself slightly. That wasn't right. It hadn't been a kiss exactly, had it? "It was more of a brief touching of lips, really."

"*A brief touching of lips*," Seeley parroted back. "What are you? A nun?"

"I don't even know how it happened." Erica covered her face with her hand. "I was trying to be friendly, trying to be funny, but he just smelled so good."

Like citrus soap mixed with spicy, heated skin.

It had been intoxicating as she'd stood there staring up into his gentle hazel eyes, his square jaw somewhat lopsided with his uncertain smile. His broad shoulders and muscular chest had been barely hidden beneath his pale blue shirt and white lab coat, making her—a strong, statuesque woman—feel delicate and feminine. In that instant, she'd wanted to fling her arms around him and have her fingers stroking through the curls of his dark brown hair as her lips smothered his. It had taken all of her self-control to stop herself from making that mistake.

"When are you going to see him again?"

"He'll be at the life drawing class on Friday."

Seeley straightened. "Then I'm coming, too."

Erica swept a hand between them, slicing the air. "No, you're not."

"It's a public class," Seeley argued. "Besides, I could be your wingwoman."

"Oh God," Erica groaned.

How had this happened? She'd been getting along swimmingly with life. Her business was booming, she'd settled, even bought a house, and she was finally content with herself and her life. Why did a man always have to come in and ruin everything?

"Now that I'm all set to meet your mystery man on Friday, why don't you just spoil the secret and tell me who he is?" Seeley's bright eyes glinted with eagerness.

"Because you probably already know him. You know everyone."

"I'm a bartender, it comes with the territory. Anyway, isn't that a good thing?" She rested her elbow on the top of the park bench and crossed a leg up on the seat as she faced Erica. "I can give you the inside goss, tell you his deepest darkest secrets. Assuming he's already told me, that is."

Erica shook her head. "I don't want to know, because I'm not interested in him."

Seeley arched a caramel eyebrow.

"I mean, nothing's going to happen between us."

"It kind of already has. It's too late to take that back."

Erica grumbled and crossed her legs, pulling her feet up underneath her on the bench. "Maybe he didn't notice."

Seeley whooped with laughter. "Yeah, a kiss is totally unnoticeable." She stared at Erica and then corrected herself. "Sorry. A *brief touching of lips*." She made air quotes with her fingers as she said the phrase.

Erica ignored her friend's sarcasm. How had things become so screwed up? This morning her life had been peachy, now it was only lunchtime and things were falling apart. It was further proof that men were the destroyers of worlds—in this case, her perfect, simple, happy, little world.

"Please." It sounded like Seeley was down to a final option—begging. "Please. Tell me now, so I know what to expect. A good wingwoman is only as good as her preparation."

"I had a little accident today," Erica began, wearily. She smoothed the fabric of the bandage covering her right knee. "I tripped and grazed the skin off my leg. It's a flesh wound really, it looked worse than it was, but Jocelyn freaked out and pretty much blackmailed me into going with her to the doctor."

Seeley poked out her tongue in disgust. "Oh my God, don't tell me it's Nate." She shivered and stuck out her tongue again. "I went to school with him. That's just—" Her face contorted with revulsion. "It's just wrong."

"That's a total overreaction. Nate seems lovely."

"Oh my God," Seeley pretended to be on the verge of vomiting. "It *is* him."

Erica huffed out a breath. "Why would you even guess it was *that* doctor's surgery Jocelyn dragged me to? There are three in the city limits."

Seeley was still gagging. "Yeah, but he's the youngest. Unless you like your men on the verge of retirement."

"That makes you wrong on two counts," Erica reproached her. "It's not Nate, and he's not the only young doctor in town."

Seeley stopped pretending to retch and pursed her lips. Then her eyes lit up in realization. "It's that new guy." She clicked her fingers as though trying to remember more information. "Mike something? No, Matt!" She beamed, her pearly-white teeth glistening. "Dr. Matt ... Matt Garrick, right?" Her tone was already a pitch above victorious.

Erica couldn't be bothered to give Seeley even more satisfaction by verbally agreeing. She picked up her sandwich from her lunchbox and stared at it, trying to ignore the fact that the unsettled feeling in her stomach was building.

"Just wait until I tell Tonya," Seeley continued, enthusiastically. "She's had her eye on him since he came to town a couple of months back. She used to obsess about him whenever we were rostered together, but now I tune it out like white noise. She's going to be super pissed she's missed her chance."

Erica nearly dropped her sandwich in surprise. "You can't tell anyone, Seels!"

Especially not that man-eater Tonya Hamilton.

Tonya was a twenty-two-year-old, bleach-blonde stunner with fake breasts and a little black book of conquests as big as a dictionary. Her doting daddy owned the largest cattle property in the Sunshine Coast Hinterlands, two restaurants in the neighboring township of Maleny, and the Montville Tavern, so she was never short on cash. Seeley had always told Erica the only reason Tonya even showed up to work was to flirt with the customers, the interstate visitors and overseas travelers in particular. If she got her perfectly-manicured claws into Matt first, there was no way Erica would consider taking her sloppy seconds.

Not that Erica was interested in Matt in that way, of course. She'd sworn off men for a while, and just because she'd had a momentary lapse of self-control, a split-second of reconsideration, didn't mean she was about to jump into a relationship with a man she knew nothing about. No, it was a matter of principle. Matt seemed like a nice guy, and Tonya ate nice guys for brunch. Erica was just concerned for his safety. That was all, honestly.

"Please." It was her turn to beg Seeley. "Don't tell anyone about this. Especially not the most eligible bachelorette in town."

"I knew you liked him." Seeley's sharp gaze and haughty grin reeked of *I told you so.*

"There's a difference between not wanting to embarrass a medical professional who's new to the region, and keeping the truth from an insatiable nymphomaniac who might ramp up her efforts of seduction if she found out."

"Yeah?" It was a scoffing sound. "And which one are you trying to do?"

Irritated, Erica uncrossed her legs and stood, walking the few steps to the trash can beside them and dumping her partially-eaten sandwich inside. When she turned back to Seeley, she made sure her glare was glacial.

"You're not coming to the class on Friday, and you're not allowed to tell anyone about the accidental lip-lock, okay?" Erica struggled to sound authoritative as she watched her friend become more amused.

Even though Seeley remained silent, the unwavering promise of mischief tugging at her features was all the answer Erica needed. Obviously, she was trying to convince the inconvincible.

CHAPTER 5

There were two beers, an out-of-date jar of black olives, a squishy avocado, a portion of cheddar cheese which had somehow become blue vein, and a bag of carrots in Matt's refrigerator. He was also pretty sure there were a couple of crusts of whole-meal bread in the freezer but knew they were likely to be moldy.

It was Thursday night, late-night shopping day if he could be bothered to put his shoes back on and leave the house, but he'd only just arrived home. He snatched a cold beer off the shelf and closed the fridge door, before using the corner of the kitchen counter to pop the top. Matt took a swig and closed his eyes, relishing the refreshing coolness and satisfyingly bitter flavor.

A *ding-dong* from the front door of his apartment had him lowering the bottle. As he wiped the back of his hand over his lips, he considered for just a moment whether or not he could ignore the interruption. He hadn't been expecting company and didn't want it. This week had been a long one so far, and, while he wasn't yet regretting the move into the nosiness of country-style living, he was definitely getting tired of all the interest he'd been receiving about his personal life.

So, he was single—big deal. He'd been that way for over a year now, and it didn't exactly mean that he must have been desperate to begin a new relationship. Nate had started something with all his wingman crap, and now every woman Matt met seemed to be either trying to set him up with someone or trying to get a date with him. It wouldn't have been so bad if the one person he was actually interested in, the one woman he couldn't stop thinking about—a certain brunette bombshell—had been the one suggested or prowling for a date, but he hadn't even seen her since that kiss. That mind-blowing kiss, like a gentle flutter of butterfly wings which had every lustful nerve in his body sparking to life. She had barely kissed him, barely touched him, but it had created a craving in him he just couldn't sate and wouldn't until his lips could meet hers again.

There was a second *ding-dong*, then an impatient third before the *thunk-thunk* of a fist against the wooden door.

"Matty-boy, open up," Nate called out cheerfully. "I know you're in there."

Matt groaned and headed for the door, beer still in hand. The compact, two-bedroom apartment he had been renting for the last two months was small enough that the kitchen-slash-dining-room-slash-living-room also happened to form the entry.

"Matt?"

There was another knock as Matt unlocked the door. He opened it to reveal Nate with a jubilant grin and a six-pack of beer.

"Sorry, we don't accept hawkers here," Matt kidded as he moved to close the door again.

Nate stopped it with a firm slap of his palm. "Don't be like that, buddy."

Matt sighed. "What do you want?"

"Thought we might have a chat." Nate held up the six-pack.

Lifting the bottle in his hand to his lips, Matt drained

every last drop of his beer before answering. "Suppose I don't get much of a choice?"

Nate's grin was at bursting point, and Matt considered there might be a risk of it splitting his friend's face if he didn't let him in. Turning in acceptance, Matt headed farther inside.

"Wait." Nate's interruption stopped Matt mid-step. "Don't you want to open your present?"

Matt spun around. What the hell was Nate talking about? What present?

Nate looked at him closely, his smile losing its glow. "Here." Stepping forward, he thrust the pack of beer into Matt's arms before disappearing back outside into the duskiness of the dim porchlight.

It only took a second for him to return with a shoebox-sized gift encased in love-heart wrapping paper.

"Someone's got an admirer," Nate sang as he closed the door behind him.

He grabbed the six-pack from Matt's hands and swapped it with the present.

"What are you talking about?" Matt glanced at the box, carefully turning it around, searching for some kind of address label, a card or, at the very least, a name scribbled on the side with pen, but there was nothing. "It's not even addressed to me, to anyone. Someone probably left it at the wrong door."

"Well, finders keepers." Nate walked past him to put the beer on the kitchen bench.

He opened the pack to grab out a warm bottle, but Matt pointed at the refrigerator.

"There's a cold one left if you want it."

"Cheers."

Nate opened the fridge, taking out the cold beer before replacing it with a few of the new ones, while Matt plopped the neatly-wrapped gift on the countertop.

"Open it."

Matt noticed Nate watching him eagerly. He took a sip

of his beer and then tipped it toward Matt as though in encouragement.

"Go on. Let's see what your secret admirer thought would win you over."

"If it's a bomb and we die standing here in this crappy kitchen, I'll haunt you for the rest of your afterlife."

Nate laughed and took another drink of his beer.

After a deep breath, digging up courage he didn't realize he needed and energy he knew for sure he was lacking, Matt began tearing at the pretty, fuchsia-colored paper, ripping love-hearts in half everywhere.

"Are they … cupcakes?" Nate was laughing again.

"Looks like red velvet," Matt agreed as he removed the rest of the wrapping paper from the clear plastic container. He cracked open the lid. "See, I told you it was left at the wrong door."

There were six of them. Six perfectly-arranged red velvet cupcakes with cream cheese frosting and an edible candy heart placed on the very top. While Matt was still gaping at the gift, trying to decide whether to attempt to rewrap it and place it in front of one of the neighboring apartments, Nate reached into the container and stole a candy heart.

"Oi," Matt snapped, closing the lid, but not quick enough to stop him. "That isn't for you."

"But apparently, it's for *you*," Nate chuckled and then stuck the heart on his tongue.

Matt frowned. They couldn't be, could they?

"I say we eat them." Nate looked ravenously at the plastic container. "I was going to suggest we order pizza, but cupcakes will do."

Matt was still drawing a blank, both on what to do with the surprise offering of baked goods and on who the gifter could possibly be. He looked at Nate, who was nearly drooling. "Do you think Melina left them?"

"In girly, pink heart paper? I doubt it. Besides, if it was her, then why wouldn't she have given you the container at work? Or me for that matter? I'm the sweets man, remember. You favor salty."

He reached for the closed container, but Matt slid it away.

"Cupcakes were meant to be eaten, Matt. You can't protect them forever."

"You help me figure out who sent them, and I'll let you have one."

"One!" Nate scoffed at him before taking another sip of his beer. "That detective work should earn me at least a half of those babies. Give me my three, and I'll write out a list of suspects. Then we have that chat I came here for, right?"

Matt shrugged. It was probably the best offer he was going to get. If they really were for him, then he wanted to thank whoever it was who'd gone through the trouble of baking them. And if they weren't and someone came knocking tomorrow, searching for their cupcakes, he'd just have to give them enough money to make a new batch.

He opened the lid and shoved the container back toward Nate, who lunged at it like a lion catching its prey.

"Okay Sherlock, start hypothesizing."

An hour later, they had run out of cupcakes and run out of ideas. Nate had gobbled down two before even scribbling out the first name on the notepad and upon finishing his third, had begged for a bonus one. Matt hadn't put up much of a fight. He'd eaten them because they were there—and because he hadn't been keen to make a meal from the ingredients in his refrigerator—but, after one and three-quarters, he was beginning to wish he had pushed harder for that pizza.

"Okay, we've agreed about taking Nicolette off the list?" Nate had his pen poised over the name to scratch it out.

Matt nodded. "I only added her because Melina has

been trying to get me to agree to go on a date with her. I doubt she even knows my name."

Nate's eyes widened. "Oh, she knows it. Melina would've been telling her about you since Tuesday when she first mentioned the possibility of a set-up." He bowed his head as he drew a line through her name. "But, I've already been on a date with her, and let me tell you, she doesn't have the culinary skills to create something like this." He tapped the empty container with the end of the pen.

There was nothing left inside except a few burgundy crumbs, five dirty cupcake liners, and the small portion of cake Matt couldn't bring himself to finish.

"That leaves us with Yasmin, Beverly, and Tonya." Nate drew a bold circle around each name.

Matt finished his third beer and took a seat at the small, four-seater dining room table, turning the chair so he could still watch Nate at the kitchen counter.

"I barely know any of those women," he told him tiredly. "I've met Tonya a couple of times, talked to Yasmin once, and Beverly is old enough to be my own mother."

"Yes," Nate agreed, pointing the end of the pen toward Matt. "But, you did meet her on speed-dating night, and you said she was very keen, too keen, about the marriage proposal business."

Matt yawned. "I think she's just lonely. I'm not one hundred percent sure she actually meant it."

"Wait a minute." Nate slapped himself lightly on the forehead. "We haven't included any guys on this list."

Matt straightened. "Are you serious?"

"We've been focusing on the women, but what about the guys in town? You know, you're likely to be Rowan's type, and I know for certain that he has decent baking skills."

Matt groaned wearily. "I give up. We've got it down to three potentials. Three *female* potentials that I don't even think have the desire or means to make me cupcakes and then leave them on my porch." He waved a hand toward the front door. "None of them even have my address."

"Yeah, but it wouldn't be too difficult for them to figure it out." Nate's expression softened sympathetically. "It's a small town, mate. Word gets around."

Matt rubbed his tired eyes. "I guess I should just appreciate the kind gesture, assuming these really were meant for me after all, and stop worrying about it."

Nate nodded in agreement. "It's different living here, Matt. Back in Brissy, it would've been unlikely that you'd ever receive a random gift like this, but here—geez, it could even be the local real estate agent trying to butter you up—who knows?"

With a long, drawn-out sigh, Matt pushed himself to his feet. "Thanks for pondering it over with me anyway, buddy. I think I'm a bit on edge about this whole dating thing, the set-up offers, the interest, that I found the surprise cupcakes a little … concerning."

Nate chuckled. "I get it. When I came back here after spending eight years at college, I thought the whole situation was disconcerting, too. But now, I'm grateful. I'm looking for something real, and it helps when you're surrounded by a whole lot of people seeking the same thing."

"Sounds like you don't need a wingman after all."

Nate just smiled. "You're not getting out of it that easily. Besides, that's why I came around in the first place. I hoped we could have a chat."

As he analyzed his friend's expression, Matt leaned a hip on the kitchen counter and crossed his arms over his chest. "A chat about what exactly?"

Eagerness filled Nate's blue-gray eyes. "The life drawing class tomorrow night."

"I've already agreed to go." Matt's cheeks warmed with the memory. "Erica asked me to attend."

She'd practically told him she wanted him around.

Come to the life drawing class … I think I'd kind of like your company.

It wasn't the best invitation he'd received, and not quite a request for a date, but it had made his heart race. Adrenalin was pumping into his veins just at the hope of spending more time with her—even though it would be doubtful they'd get to spend any of it alone together.

"Really? Good for you, mate. It's about time someone caught your eye. So, you won't mind talking to her for me then?"

Something dropped heavily in Matt's gut. Nate wasn't interested in Erica, too, was he? Matt couldn't bear to compete with his best friend in the fight for Erica's heart—mainly because he knew for sure that Nate would win.

His tongue felt too thick in his mouth, and he swallowed nervously. "About what?"

Nate hissed in a breath and took a moment before he met Matt's gaze again. "It's stupid, but … I thought we might persuade her to organize a nighttime class for a certain age group. You know, like a class for those who are thirty-five and under?"

Matt released the gulp of air he'd been holding. "I'm guessing they'll also have to be single and female to meet the class requirements?"

Nate offered him an innocent shrug. "Sure. That'd be helpful."

"She had a feeling you'd try to do something like this. Erica, I mean. I think she could sense your desperation when she met you on Tuesday."

"I am not desperate," Nate sniffed. "I just don't want to waste my time. I'm almost thirty-one and haven't had one decent long-term relationship."

"Do you think that could have something to do with the fact that, until recently, your concept of long-term involved texting them the morning after?"

"What? I like to try before I buy, and I've just never

found one that I wanted to pay the money for."

Matt groaned and raised a hand to cover his eyes. "You can be a real ass, you know that?"

"Come on," Nate argued, "you know what I mean. I like all women, we have good times together, but it's the love that eludes me. Those good times used to be enough, but now I want something more. You can't criticize me for that."

Lowering his hand, Matt looked at Nate. He understood what his buddy meant, even if he hadn't put it as eloquently or politically correct as he should have. The sincerity in Nate's usually-jovial countenance said it all. He had grown up—maybe not a whole lot, and maybe not as much as he should have in his lifetime, but he'd grown up—enough to know that he wanted to find his other half, that big love those who are happily married often talk about. Matt knew his friend wanted to share his life, his happiness with someone who meant the world to him. Nate just hadn't found her yet, and sometimes, maybe like Matt himself, Nate probably wondered if he ever would.

Matt's thoughts wandered back to Erica, that long dark hair, the sun-kissed tan of her soft skin, those dreamy coffee-brown eyes, and he breathed out another sigh. As he inhaled, he imagined he caught the scent of her. *Strawberries and vanilla.* His mouth watered.

If he didn't go to bed soon and let the emptiness of sleep consume him, distract him, he'd need another beer.

"Okay." Matt nodded.

"Really, buddy?"

"I can't promise anything, but I'll see what I can do. I can only suggest it, right? And if she says no, then it's a no."

Nate grinned as he picked up his half-empty bottle of beer from the countertop. He pointed the spout at Matt. "I knew there was a reason I dubbed you my wingman."

CHAPTER 6

"Same again?" Seeley had her hand poised above Erica's empty glass.

Erica shook her head. "I mainly dropped in for a catch-up, since we couldn't meet for lunch today."

"You mean, you dropped in to set the rules for tomorrow night?" Seeley stared at her from the other side of the bar in the Montville Tavern, her haughty expression revealing her shrewd understanding. "I'm guessing you want to tell me what I am and am not allowed to do at the life drawing class."

Erica nibbled at her lower lip. She couldn't deny the allegation. She'd come here tonight to do exactly that.

"It's not that I don't want you there," Erica began.

"Yeah," Seeley coughed out a laugh.

"I'm serious, Seels. I'm glad you're coming."

She hadn't really been thrilled at the prospect in the beginning, but having had the last couple of days to ruminate over it had made her realize that safety lay in numbers. Erica hadn't been able to stop thinking about Matt, to stop imagining what may have happened if she'd kissed him deeper, stayed a bit longer. It had haunted her dreams, both in sleep and while awake. She'd somehow let him get under her skin, and that was a very dangerous thing.

Seeley looked at her closely. "You really mean that?"

Erica nodded. "It'll be easier with you there."

Maybe there would be less chance of her doing something she'd regret, something intimate with Matt, if Seeley was watching?

"I can't believe you're happy for me to come, even though I'm rubbish at sketching and even worse at keeping my nose out of your business." She shot Erica a look of suspicion. "Is there another reason why you're now inviting me?"

"Inviting you to what?" Tonya, all five feet, five inches of her, stalked from the other side of the bar to stand beside Seeley.

Her stylishly manicured hand went to her curvy hip and she smiled sweetly, causing an attractive little dimple to appear on her right cheek.

Seeley, who similarly towered above Tonya at five feet, nine as Erica did at five feet, ten, glanced down at the busty, bleach-blonde. "Oh, nothing, Ton," she lied with a shake of her head. "We were just talking about Erica's art class."

Tonya grinned excitedly. "I heard it's supposed to be a special night tomorrow."

Erica grimaced and then used a nearby coaster to slap the hand Seeley had left resting on the bar counter. "Have you told everyone?"

"Ow!" Seeley pulled her hand away. "Hold on a second."

Tonya looked confused. "Beverly told me. She heard it from Samuel, who heard it from Jocelyn. Apparently, the boys from the Hoffman Close Medical Practice will be there."

"And what makes that special?" Seeley remained unmoved.

Tonya huffed exasperatedly. "Are you serious? All the

single women of a certain age in town are going. Those boys are tall, good-looking, with thick hair, and all their own teeth, not to mention they're both doctors. Word spread like head lice through a kindergarten."

"Eww," Seeley interrupted with a sound of distaste, which garnered her a smirk from Tonya.

"I'm pretty sure everyone who'd want to know would already know by now."

Erica threw her hands up. "And how are all these people supposed to fit in my classroom? I'll be lucky to squeeze in thirty at best, but I only have equipment for twenty-five."

Tonya shrugged. "Guess you better figure something out quick."

"Thanks," Erica snipped before turning back to Seeley. "Shit."

The hushed word had Seeley's eyes widening. "We'll figure something out, Erica. It'll be fine." She gestured to Erica's plain navy T-shirt with its odd speck of colored paint, forcing Erica's attention to follow. "We could stick you in that sparkly halter top you only bring out for special occasions. It really puts your girls on show."

Tonya held up a hand. "Wait. Am I missing something?" She studied Seeley then Erica. "You invited them because *you're* interested?"

"No. I—" After struggling to find the right words, Erica picked up the coaster and moved to slap Seeley with it again, but this time Seeley saw it coming and backed up.

"Not my fault." The tinge of guilt in Seeley's own voice said otherwise.

Tonya winked. "Good on you, Erica. I didn't realize you had it in you. You're always alone, so I just assumed you had some kind of hideous disfigurement underneath the art smock."

"Actually, I was taking a break from men." Erica's eyes widened as she caught her own mistake. "I *am* taking a break ... and *I* didn't invite *them*."

Well, she hadn't really. Technically she'd only invited Matt, but Tonya didn't need to know that.

As Erica gave Seeley a look of warning, Seeley thinned her lips, pressing them tightly together as though suggesting no more secrets would escape through them. When Erica returned her attention to Tonya, she realized the younger woman had been observing the exchange with interest.

Erica opened her mouth to explain—well, lie—but Tonya raised a hand in her direction.

"Don't worry, hon. My lips are sealed, too." Her dimple returned as she smiled. "You know, I was reminded only yesterday that the best way to a man's heart is through his stomach."

"Yeah, that's why you work here, Ton," Seeley whooped. "Give them beer and everything's peachy."

"I was going to suggest that Erica have some finger food at this particular class, that maybe it would help make the boys more … compliant, but beer would totally work, too."

"Thanks for that pearl of wisdom." Seeley's eyes flashed impishly.

"Anytime," Tonya told her as she turned on her heel and headed back to the other side of the bar to remove the dirty glasses a couple of middle-aged men had left behind.

Seeley watched her go and then leaned closer to Erica, resting her elbows on the supple rubber of the bar runner. "I've got your back," she whispered. "I'm in good with the science teacher at Montville Elementary. I can get you a few extra desks, but you might want to start rationing paintbrushes."

"That might not be enough. By the sound of it, I should be prepared to turn people away at the door."

"Guess I need to make sure I get there early then?"

"You? Early? Has the world fallen off its axis?"

"Yeah, yeah." Seeley straightened. "I was going to say you could borrow my leather minidress, make that man of yours drool, but now I don't think I will."

Erica spat out a laugh. "He's not *my* man, Seels. Besides, I'd be flat-out fitting into something of yours." Her hands hovered over her plump breasts as though that offered enough explanation.

Seeley tossed her head in feigned offense, making her uneven caramel bangs fly. "That's the whole point." Then she beamed wholeheartedly, unable to keep up the façade. "Is it wrong that I'm excited?"

When Erica nodded, Seeley ignored her.

"So, what'll we be drawing? A bowl of fruit, a vase of flowers … a naked man?"

"What kind of class do you think you're coming to?"

"Apparently a boring one."

"I've got a female model lined up," Erica explained, refusing to acknowledge her friend's previous comment. "It's not a nude, but it should still be interesting. Last week I promised the class a mythological theme, so I've arranged for Yasmin to pose as an ancient Greek goddess."

Seeley stuck out her tongue, clearly unimpressed. "Yasmin?"

Erica nodded. "She's one of a few people in town willing to model for free."

"That's because it's *Yasmin*," Seeley huffed. "Any attention is good attention to her."

"She's a sweetheart." Erica glared at her. "Is there anyone in town you don't have a problem with?"

Seeley's smile turned sickly sweet. "You. Bestie."

Erica grabbed the coaster again, poising to slap Seeley's hand, but before she could follow through, Seeley snatched it from between her fingers.

"I'm going to have to ban these things," she warned her, tossing it over her shoulder and onto the floor behind the bar counter.

CHAPTER 7

Erica ran for the ringing telephone, nearly dropping the bucket of paintbrushes in her hand as she did so. If it was yet another person calling to make a last-minute booking into tonight's life drawing class, she would probably hang up on them and unplug the phone completely. Well, that or tell them to go get stuffed. But neither one of those options, especially the latter, would be a positive for her business, so out of habit rather than increased patience, she picked up the phone and answered politely.

"Hello, you've reached Unique Art Boutique. It's Erica speaking."

"Hi, Erica." As Yasmin's husky voice met her ear, Erica breathed a sigh of relief.

She offered Seeley a reassuring wave as she noticed her glance up from where they'd been arranging the borrowed school desks with the help of Tom Mathers, the nerdy but adorable science teacher from Montville Elementary. Poor Tom had nurtured his crush on Seeley for years, but from what she frequently told Erica, he just wasn't her type. Unfortunately for him, his lack of a Harley Davidson and a womanizing attitude were notches against his favor.

"It's only Yasmin," she called out to them.

Tom smiled in acknowledgment, his eyes cheerful behind his thin-rimmed glasses as he shifted a small desk into place, while Seeley poked out her tongue.

Ignoring Seeley's unnecessary rudeness, Erica returned her attention to the telephone. "I guess we'll be seeing you shortly then? It's going to be a busy night, so I'll make sure you get a couple of extra breaks if you need them."

"I should've called in earlier," Yasmin began. "I'm so sorry, Erica, but I'm not well. I won't be able to make it tonight."

Erica heard the unsettling tremble in Yasmin's concerned voice, and suddenly the events of the coming evening, all the preparation and stress, didn't seem as important anymore.

"Are you okay?" Erica's gaze dropped to the tidy counter in front of her as she listened intently for an answer.

"I've been very ill." She sounded on the verge of tears. "Food poisoning, I think. Dr. Lutinski from the Main Street Clinic is on call for home visits and will be coming around soon, but apparently it's been a hectic day for him, as well."

"You poor thing," Erica murmured as she placed a cool hand over her eyes. "Don't worry about things here, Yas. We've got it covered. Thanks for calling in though. I hope you feel better soon."

After Yasmin sobbed out a good-bye, Erica lowered her hand from her face and disconnected the call. She checked the lit screen of the cordless phone, noting she had just under an hour to contact the two other women she had retained as life models in the past. With a calming breath, she flicked through the little black book of contact details she kept beside the phone and then punched in the first woman's number.

"What's going on?"

Seeley was standing beside her, concern contorting her angular features. Erica hadn't even noticed her leave the classroom, hadn't been paying attention to the *thud* of her boots on the wooden floorboards. She gazed at her friend, weariness making her sigh, as she listened to the first ring.

"Yasmin's sick."

Seeley perked up at the announcement, provoking Erica's irritation.

"Don't you dare." She pointed a finger in Seeley's direction as the ringing on the phone line continued. "Unless you're going to help me find someone else at the last minute or you're willing to model yourself, don't say another word."

"I think this may be a blessing in disguise." Seeley spoke carefully as though she were anticipating a violent reaction.

Erica gritted her teeth, forcing herself to ignore the sudden urge she had to search the countertop for a weapon as the phone line clicked over into voicemail. Without the patience or clarity of mind to leave a suitable message, she removed the phone from her ear and disconnected the call.

Obviously seeing no sign of retaliation, Seeley continued, "I think *you* should be the one to model."

Erica just blinked at her. "I'm sorry, what?" Her tone was thick with sarcasm.

She looked over at Tom, partly seeking support in her astonishment and outrage, and partly because she was sure her brash reaction would've drawn his attention. He appeared unfazed, his rangy body bent as he dragged a table into place while his neatly-styled dark hair barely quivered with the movement. Yet, Erica was almost certain he was glancing their way, his eyes stretching to catch a glimpse of the drama in his peripheral vision. When she looked back at Seeley, the confident grin on her friend's face irked her.

"You can't be serious, Seels? Who would take the class?"

"I can do it. Just tell me what you want me to say."

"No," Erica scoffed and shook her head, but she knew the word itself didn't sound concrete. "No," she said again, more brusquely.

Seeley waved a hand at the cordless phone. "Fine. Make your calls. I just think tonight would go a whole lot better with you out there on display. Can you think of a better way to keep Matt's attention focused on you instead of the other hussies intruding on tonight's event?"

Erica hadn't thought of it like that. Maybe she should be the one modeling after all? Did she really want Matt ogling another woman posing provocatively in a sheer, Grecian-inspired nightgown? She shook the sudden wave of jealousy away. What was wrong with her? She was supposed to be on a man-free diet. Matt was not hers, and she didn't want him. Did she?

She smirked at Seeley. "Are you lumping yourself into the same category, Seels?"

Seeley offered her a glare, but Erica was undaunted.

"*Intruding hussy,*" she continued slowly as though feeling out the words with her tongue. "Sounds just like you."

"Anyone ever tell you you're a terrible friend?" Seeley threw the retort over her shoulder as she stalked away back toward the classroom, but after a few steps, she glanced back at Erica and winked her approval.

Satisfied, Erica hit redial on the cordless phone and lifted it to her ear.

CHAPTER 8

"Look, I know this is totally sexist of me, but I've got to say it." Nate spread his hands in a gesture that encompassed the entire classroom. "What a smorgasbord of honeys."

Matt rubbed a hand over his eyes. He had reached a point well beyond regret. He should never have come, he could barely draw a stick figure, and the only reason he'd even agreed to attend in the first place was yet to show her beautiful face.

Nate, on the other hand, was a ball of excitement and anticipation. He was clearly more than ready to let the action begin, and by *action*, he'd been quite blatant in referring to the time he was keen to spend chatting up the ladies rather than creating a work of art.

"What's up with you?" Nate's question was accompanied by a firm *whack* to Matt's shoulder.

Matt lowered the hand from his suddenly tired eyes and gazed over the array of young, local women smiling eagerly at him. Each of them had already taken a seat at the prepared range of painting easels and individual tables that circled around a short, rectangular-shaped stage, leaving only two free easels on either side of the room. Some of the women had begun motioning to the empty seats, their gaze fixed to his, lashes fluttering, come-hither looks dialed to full power.

The intensity of being the center of attention was making Matt's skin prickle and his stomach churn. Although he and Nate were still standing at the invisible threshold that separated the art store side of the shop from the classroom, Matt wasn't yet brave enough to take that final step and didn't know when he might be ready to. His brain was working hard trying to reassure him that he wasn't in any danger, but his natural instincts had triggered his fight or flight mode, and running was starting to sound like the best option. He had just about made his mind up to turn around and head back out the front door when Nate draped an arm around his shoulders, crinkling his gray shirt and removing all opportunity for escape.

"Get it together, buddy," Nate murmured through gritted teeth. "They can smell your fear."

"Yeah, like a pack of starving hyenas." Matt tilted his head closer to his friend, careful to whisper. "Remind me why I'm doing this again?"

Matt sensed more than saw Nate's grin.

"Because you're a great friend, an awesome wingman, and you've got a huge selfless heart, which thrives on doing favors for your best bud."

Matt choked back a laugh as he returned his gaze to their audience. Their female peers had decided to increase their attempts to lure them farther inside with some now standing and heading toward them. Matt's heartrate sped, fearful adrenalin coursing through his veins causing his palms to dampen. He made a subtle move to hide the obvious sign of fear by smoothing his hands over his black work slacks. Surely it had to be safer to run than stay and fight off these lionesses.

"Get your butts back in those seats!" The growl of an order came from a skinny young woman with a choppy, dark-blonde bob at the back of the room.

The few women standing paused in their pursuit, glowering their disapproval at the other taller woman before reluctantly returning to their chairs.

"Seeley Cabot," Nate muttered, nodding toward the fierce woman. "She's always been a hard-ass."

Seeley crossed her arms and scowled across the room at them. "Are you two losers going to take a seat, or am I going to have to make you?"

Among the hushed, chastising grumbles from around the classroom, Matt heard the sweet tones of a familiar female voice.

"Seels!"

It may have been only one word uttered with ferocious reproach, but it was like a siren's song to his ears, to his heart. It was enough to have his feet moving, dragging him across the wooden floor to the nearest vacant easel.

She was here. Erica was here as promised, and now there was a much more important reason for him to stay.

As Matt took his seat, he noticed Nate do the same opposite him across the small stage, lapping up the female attention as he did so. While the women nearest to Matt pawed at him, murmuring introductions, he couldn't tear his gaze free of the scarlet curtain hanging behind Seeley, concealing the far corner of the room. He was almost positive the melodious sound of Erica's voice had emanated from behind that fabric. He stared at it, hoping he might be able to will her out of hiding.

"Okay," Seeley announced, walking toward the center stage. "Now that everyone's finally ready to begin, shall we reveal our guest of honor?"

The women in the room appeared puzzled as they dragged their attention from him and Nate to stare at her. Apparently, they were under the impression their *guests* of honor had already arrived. It took him a brief moment, but Matt quickly sparked onto her meaning.

The guest of honor for a life drawing class? That had to be the model, didn't it? And once the model made his or her entrance, then so, too, would the art teacher.

He ignored Seeley to focus on the gentle sway of the crimson curtain. He wanted to tell her to ditch the anticipation and bring the goddam model out already so he could start playing teacher's pet. But, before he could utter a word, the sudden shifting of the curtain had him holding his breath instead.

The scarlet fabric drew to the side in one fluid motion, revealing—to everyone's gasps of surprise—an absolute angel.

Matt felt his heart stop. He couldn't breathe. He was completely captivated, his eyes wide as a voracious desire sparked to life within him.

Erica strode gracefully toward the stage, the sheer snowflake-white chiffon of the elegant Grecian-inspired nightgown flowing around her delectable curves with each step. Only the snug cream-colored corset and matching panties ensured she retained a minuscule of modesty. Her long, dark brown hair cascaded down her shoulders like chocolate silk, while shorter tendrils curled over her cheekbones. Her gorgeous features were further enhanced by neatly-applied makeup, giving her eyes a sensual smolder and making her already-sexy mouth unbearably erotic. The mocha of her silky-looking skin provided a stunning contrast to the glow of her outfit, proving to everyone in the audience that the magnificent nightgown was clearly made for her incredible body. As she stepped up on the stage, her bare feet sliding across the black felt-covered surface, her coffee brown eyes lifted to meet Matt's.

His breath caught in his throat at the sight of the sexiest woman he'd ever seen giving him the world's most sensual smile. Matt's heart pounded in a suddenly chaotic rhythm, and another sharp intake of air left him spluttering, choking on his own saliva, unable to catch his breath without making a further ass of himself.

All the class members whose gaze had been firmly

fixed on Erica's entrance quickly turned their attention to his attack of idiocy, with some of them even hurrying to his aid. Deep embarrassment had Matt's head lowering as he continued coughing, desperately dragging in air, until he heard Nate's laughter. He glared in his friend's direction, his breathing slowly calming as one of the women beside him offered him a cup of water. He took it appreciatively, noting Nate's feigned innocence before he turned back to the familiar-looking young woman beside him.

"Thank you." His words croaked out.

"You're welcome." Her kind smile reached her friendly emerald green eyes as she slipped her fingers nervously through the side of her blonde pixie-cut hairstyle.

Matt took a deep drink and finally began to feel less like an imbecile. His face was warm from the flush of humiliation and the fact that his inability to be suave had almost killed him. Braving a glance at the stage, he noticed Erica watching him out of the corner of her eye as she positioned herself in a lounging pose, one long, shapely leg stretched out before her while the other remained bent. A wicked smirk teased at the corners of her luscious mouth as she leaned back on one hand and held the other cupped out in front of her. When her long black lashes finally lifted and her exquisite brown eyes met his, Matt had to work hard to control his reaction.

I will not make an ass of myself again. I will not make an ass of myself again.

Maybe if he said it over and over in his head a few more times it would actually happen. He breathed and the world kept turning. He didn't cough or faint or fall over or do anything else that might have made him appear like an even bigger idiot than he already was.

Relaxing, Matt offered Erica a smile, knowing all too well it was tinged with the slightest bit of pride.

"Well, that got an even better reaction than I expected," Seeley quipped sassily as she placed a small, intricately-painted terracotta bowl in Erica's open palm.

"Everyone's clearly happy with the choice of model then."

Even though she'd posed it as an obvious statement and not a question, a couple of younger women from the inner circle of easels and desks grumbled their disagreement. Seeley shot them a harsh glare.

"Correction. Everyone who matters."

Matt noticed several disgruntled expressions as Seeley turned away from her opponents and walked outside the circle. When she spun back around, a taunting grin brightened her eyes.

"Shall we begin?"

CHAPTER 9

Erica's bottom was so numb she was starting to wonder if it had somehow fused to the stage. Either that, or maybe it had melted from the pressure of holding up the rest of her body for so long and was now evaporating into the air. From the spikes of pain spreading down her shoulder to her wrist, she was also pretty sure her arm was about to drop off. At least the pain of maintaining the same position for such a lengthy period of time had helped her discover a newfound respect for her life drawing models.

Moving only her eyes, she risked a peek down at the knee she'd left bent, thinking once again what a good job Seeley had done hiding the scabs of her wound with a couple of skin-colored sticky bandages and some cleverly-applied makeup. Although the gash itself had mostly healed, there were still a couple of bruises that would take a little longer. As it was, with her arm in agony and her butt aching from numbness, Erica was worried she'd end up with even more injuries after this hardship.

Seeley had promised her another break over an hour ago, but considering how *well* the last one had gone, Erica doubted she'd follow through. When Seeley had called a halt to the sketching for a measly fifteen minutes, women everywhere had begun throwing themselves at Nate and Matt. Such a ruckus had ensued and a scary level of antagonism had grown, that Matt had actually asked her for help. Yet, as she'd taken a step toward him, having stood to stretch out her body before beginning another long stint of being a living mannequin, the women surrounding Matt had quickly blocked her path. Fortunately, Seeley had seen the interaction and yelled at everyone, telling them to return to their seats before things could escalate.

At the time, Erica had been stunned by the jealousy which had overwhelmed her. She'd never felt like that before, so protective, possessive. It probably hadn't helped that Seeley had talked her ear off all afternoon about how there would be such a competition among the women in the class to win the attention of the guys. It was because of their conversation that Erica had actually gotten to the point where she'd concurred with Seeley, agreeing that the idea of having *her* model might be the best option.

Apparently, a bout of food poisoning was going around town. All of her models had claimed to be victims of the illness. Erica would've wondered if Seeley had played some part in it, had she not heard several of the women in the class talking about how their own friends had been struck down with the same affliction. In the end, Seeley's answer to the problem had been Erica's only solution and some mischievous part of her, the part which didn't quite understand the whole "break from men" concept, had been thoroughly excited.

Now, however, with her numb bottom and the pain of pins and needles shooting through her raised arm, Erica was starting to think that the whole thing hadn't been such a great idea after all.

Her gaze met Seeley's across the room, and she watched as her friend yawned audibly, stretching her skinny limbs in her tight blue jeans and indigo singlet.

Even though it was obvious Seeley was genuinely tired, Erica mentally cursed her for flouting her ability to move so freely. Both of them were lacking patience, utterly exhausted, and so, it seemed, was Matt. Only Nate and the twenty-eight single women in the room were still exuberant and peppy after over two hours of artistry. Erica peered through the wall of shelving, which separated the store from the classroom, to check the clock above the service counter, careful to only move her eyes, while keeping the rest of her body as still as she could manage.

Make that two and a half hours.

A normal class would have finished by now, most were no longer than two, but Erica had told Seeley to give everyone a little more time this session. She'd expected a lot of distracted students after all the hype surrounding the guys' attendance, and also anticipated a lot of the newer students—those who had likely only come for the dating opportunity—wouldn't yet have the skills to complete a significant amount of work in the allotted time. She was now seriously regretting making that decision. Who gave a crap if her new students couldn't finish their artwork or not? Surely the ability to retain functionality in her arm and the well-being of her backside was way more important.

"Okay, that's it, everybody. Pencils down." Seeley's brash, authoritative tone was tinged with weariness.

There were some groans from the crowd, even more sounds of relief as people began to lower their pencils and look over at their classmates and the artwork around them. Erica had observed that this last segment had been more productive than the first, with more than half the class finally showing a substantial amount of interest in their task. It had probably helped that Nate had announced during their brief break that he'd always had a thing for creative women. Whether he'd done it to take the heat off of him and Matt, help Seeley keep the class in line, or made the comment for selfish reasons in an effort to narrow down the field of potential partners, Erica just didn't know. Either way, it had helped.

A light hum of chatter rumbled through the room as Erica lowered the terracotta bowl to the stage and forced her body out of the pose she'd earlier thought comfortable. Muscles ached, complaining with the movement, somewhere in her spine a bone cracked pleasantly back into place, and as she got to her feet, both her blood and her own hands rushed down to her backside.

Yep. Still there. There'd been no butt-fusing, no butt-melting, the plump roundness of it remained—making her suddenly wish the effort of her unpleasant experience could at the very least have made the whole thing a bit smaller.

She chose that instant, with her hands still grasping the firmness of her cheeks, to glance over at Matt. He was staring at her as he had throughout the whole class.

She'd purposely held her head straight when she'd arranged herself in the modeling pose, keeping her gaze away from the very distraction that was Dr. Matthew Garrick, and yet, she'd seen him eyeing her from her peripheral vision. It shouldn't have felt odd. She had been on display for the whole class, after all. She was supposed to be their muse, they were supposed to be ogling her. Yet, it felt different with Matt. Electricity had sparked, crackling in the air between them, while a fiery heat had radiated from him, from the whole of his body to hers.

Erica could feel that heat now as she stared at him, drowning in the molten depths of his hazel eyes, his sensual look holding her hostage. Her skin prickled, goosebumps formed, and her nipples hardened with the electricity, the astounding chemistry that vibrated between them.

He looked hungry, his tongue slipping out to wet his lips as he watched her hands slide from her backside, over her hips, and up the sturdy cream-colored corset to stop just below her breasts.

Erica could hear the women around Matt talking to him, saying his name, reminding him of theirs, but he never uttered a word as his eyes remained locked to hers.

He was such an incredibly handsome man. Erica was sure Seeley would have her own criticisms. She would say that his dark hair, which curled over his ears and the base of his neck, was too long, that his features were chiseled but not quite angular enough, that there was a softness to them, a kindness, a gentleness to his eyes, a natural cheerfulness in the curving of his lips that made him seem too friendly, too hot-guy-next-door for her bad-boy appetites. Knowing Seeley, Matt would need to be a skinhead with a sleeve tattoo and an eyebrow piercing to have caught her interest. Luckily for Erica, she thought he was unbelievably perfect just the way he was.

It took a moment for her to realize she was smiling at him, that he was smiling at her, and that all the women around him had shut up to stare at them both.

"A-ah-um." A sudden attack of nerves had Erica stuttering, searching for something to say.

Cool fingers slipped around her arm, and she was abruptly dragged toward the edge of the stage. Seeley's grouchy voice erupted beside her.

"You can all clear out. Class is officially finished for the evening. Feel free to take your artworks home, and remember, if you had a good time tonight, the life drawing class is on at the same time every Friday night."

Chairs scraped against the floorboards, and cheerful feminine chatter echoed through the room as numerous members of the class stood and began to leave. Only a dedicated few made it clear they had every intention of remaining. Nicolette, the big-boned, ashen-blonde, who also happened to be the local minister's daughter, was doing her darnedest to steal Nate's attention away from Chloe and Anabelle, the petite, brunette non-identical twins who frequented the pottery class Erica held every Wednesday.

"Thanks for the save," Erica told Seeley appreciatively.

"All good." Her friend gave her a small smile and then nodded in Matt's direction. "I was worried they might tear you to shreds if you kept staking such an obvious claim."

"Hey," Erica snapped. "Looking is not the same thing as claiming."

As Seeley shrugged, Erica followed her friend's gaze back to where Tonya was now leaning over Matt, her buxom chest propped in front of his face while she caressed his shoulder flirtatiously with her sharp but elegant manicure. Lauren and another woman with tight black curls and an enviably small backside were hovering nearby, observing Tonya's display with intense disappointment. Obviously irritated, the other woman made a hurried move toward Matt and Tonya, before Lauren laid a gentle hand on her shoulder. Erica saw Lauren whisper something to her, calming her, until the other woman nodded and retreated.

Lauren suddenly looked their way and offered them a wide, friendly grin. "Thanks for tonight, Erica. We had a lovely time."

Erica smiled her gratitude as Lauren and her raven-haired friend waved good-bye, then headed for the front door.

"Thank heavens for Lauren," Seeley said quietly. "I thought we were about to witness a murder."

Erica frowned, watching the two women exit the building as the *tinkle* of the little bell above the entrance declared their departure. "Who was the woman with her? I feel like I've seen her before."

"That's Diana Parker. She's been friends with Lauren since kindergarten, but you've probably seen her working at the Montville Information Center."

Erica clicked her fingers triumphantly. "That's it."

"She's usually pretty chill, but when it comes to a competition, she's not someone you want to mess with. In tenth grade, she supposedly broke some girl's tibia during the hockey finals."

"Geez," Erica exhaled the word in a long sigh.

Seeley nodded. "Yep."

A squeak of a chair against the floorboards drew their attention over to Nate, who was rising to his feet, one non-identical twin on each arm, while Nicolette flittered about in front of him as though trying to decide which appendage was hers to hang on to. Nate was smug with satisfaction as he looked over to where Matt was still copping an eyeful of Tonya's bosom. Although Matt's smile had a politeness about it, there was an underlying air of uncertainty, an anxiousness about him that made Erica suspect he wasn't as comfortable as his buddy was with the attention he was receiving.

"Not to interrupt your fun, love birds," Nate ribbed Matt and Tonya, "but, we're heading over to the Montville Tavern for a few drinks. Want to join?"

Matt's handsome eyes grew large, and he shook his head.

Tonya straightened to face Nate and his companions. "We'd love to," she told them.

Nate laughed as Tonya grabbed Matt, tugging him up from his seat.

"It's getting late," Matt told her, remaining polite throughout the dismissal. "It's nearly ten. I think it might be best if I called it a night."

Tonya just giggled and yanked him closer to her. "Come on, grandpa. Another hour and a couple of shots of tequila won't kill you."

Matt cast a worried look at Erica.

She wanted to help him, wanted to tell him to choose her, to spend the time in her company instead. Maybe even spend the night together? But, this sinfully-attractive man wasn't hers. To have him, she would likely need to submit to a serious relationship and that was something she wasn't yet ready for. So, no, she wouldn't stop him from sharing shots with Tonya, from spending time with any other woman, even though she might want to. He wasn't hers to be stopped. He was entitled to seek out a potential partner who could love him the way he deserved to be loved.

Erica ignored the fire of jealousy building in her gut and offered the room a kind smile. "Thanks for coming tonight, everyone. I hope it lived up to your expectations and that I might see some, if not all, of you here next week." She met Matt's stare again, and pushed the hope in her words into her eyes.

As though he'd understood her meaning, Matt beamed, but before he could utter a word, Tonya began dragging him toward the static shelving that separated the two spaces of the store.

"That's for sure, Erica. It's been a blast." Nate headed after them, the twins still on each arm as Nicolette trailed close behind.

When Tonya and Matt neared the front door, her fingers like a white-knuckled vice around his arm, Matt shot another helpless look at Erica.

"I'll definitely be back," he called out.

Then Tonya opened the front door, the little bell *tinkling*, and yanked him through it.

Chloe and Anabelle waved as they departed with Nate, Nicolette hot on their heels, and then they were all alone— just Erica, her best friend, and a whole lot of mess.

"Come on, I'll give you a hand cleaning up." Seeley motioned to the circle of easels and school desks, the paper and pencils, some scattered across the floor, and the randomly scattered plastic cups of water that had been provided.

Erica placed a hand on her arm before Seeley could attempt to tidy anything.

"Let's leave it until the morning. I'm tired, and class is at ten tomorrow, so I'll have plenty of time to get things in order by then."

Seeley eyed her a little suspiciously. "Really? You know I don't mind."

Erica chuckled, but exhaustion clipped the joyous sound short. "Really, Seels. I know you'd love to hang around and discuss the ins and outs of this evening, but I'm just not up to it."

"Okay," She nodded in understanding. "I'll head home on one condition: we meet up sometime tomorrow for a debrief?"

"Fine." Erica yawned. "I'll give you a call."

"You better." Seeley patted Erica's arm reassuringly before heading for the exit.

After watching her friend round the open shelving and walk toward the front door, Erica released a deep sigh.

"You know he wants you."

Seeley's bold statement brought Erica's attention back to her friend. As they stared across the room at each other, Seeley's lips quirked and her perceptive eyes twinkled with mischief.

"Just saying." She shrugged almost innocently and then reached for the door handle.

The little bell at the entrance *tinkled* happily as the door opened and Seeley stepped outside.

CHAPTER 10

"Just a minute," Erica called as the knocking at the front door to the Unique Art Boutique continued.

She had nearly gotten her pants on. She slid the denim shorts over her hips and pushed aside the crimson curtain, hurrying through the classroom as she zipped and buttoned the shorts in place.

Again, someone pounded hard on the front door.

"Coming," she yelled as she skipped around the shelves and dashed for the entrance.

She had no idea who it could have been, especially at this time of night, but since the life drawing class had finished half an hour ago, common sense suggested that someone had returned to collect something they'd accidentally left behind.

Self-consciousness had Erica draping an arm over her chest in an effort to hide the copious amount of cleavage created by the corset. When she'd sent Seeley home earlier, she hadn't had the foresight to realize just how difficult it would be to free herself from the evil contraption. She'd already spent a great deal of time tugging at it, pulling at the laces, but had only succeeded in knotting it up tighter. If worse came to worst, she would end up sleeping in the damn thing or cutting it off.

She used her thumb to snap open the lock then pulled the door inward.

"Yes?" She was a little breathless, flustered by her rush to answer the late caller.

Erica glanced up, following the mass of masculine chest beneath the soft fabric of a gray business shirt to a neat collar revealing a strong neck. There was a square jaw slightly lopsided by a satisfied smile on full lips, then a straight nose, before an attractive pair of friendly hazel eyes caught her stare. Eyes that seemed to beam at her, their irises churning with flecks of gold, emerald, and chocolate, turning molten as they looked down, taking in her appearance.

"I told you I'd come back." Matt's deep voice was husky as though burdened, struggling for control.

She gasped in surprise. "I didn't realize you'd meant tonight. I assumed you had other *things* planned."

She wanted to ask about Tonya, wanted to know who had left whom and why, but thought better of it. It wasn't her business; Matt and Tonya could do as they pleased and it wouldn't matter to her, would it?

Matt shook his head. "No. No plans except these."

His gaze rose to hers, and the desire she saw there, the lust that had those handsome eyes darkening, tugged at something deep in her gut, at the core of her being.

He took a step toward her, over the threshold, and she stepped back, releasing the door to him, inviting him in with a non-verbal request.

"You are so incredibly gorgeous." He exhaled the words as though he couldn't restrain their release.

She laughed sharply. "It's the makeup."

Matt shook his head again, then closed the door behind him. "I wanted to help you clean up, maybe we could talk as we did so. I'd …" He paused, his brow furrowing. "I'd really like to get to know you better."

For an instant, Erica had imagined he'd come back, his

body seeking hers, searching to fulfill that desperate need their unique attraction had sparked between them. She'd known Seeley was right, Matt wanted her, just as much as Erica wanted him, but that didn't mean they had to do anything about it. Besides the fact that they wanted different things, that they were at different stages in their lives—him, possibly wanting to settle down; her, needing to focus on herself and her career—they were also adults, after all, and they could keep their minds in control of their bodies.

"Sure." Erica's heart jumped to her throat. "I'd like to get to know you better, too."

She turned, walking back toward the classroom, sensing the heat of his body, his nearness, following close behind her.

"I'd planned to leave this until morning," she continued, gesturing to the mess left over from the life drawing class. "But, if you're certain you'd like to help, then I'd really appreciate it."

"Of course. You shouldn't have to do all of this by yourself."

Erica shrugged—the hand on her shoulder bobbing with the movement—shifting the arm covering the expanse of bare cleavage just a little. The motion made her once more aware of her indecency, and she became determined to escape the confines of the snug torture device.

"I usually do, but it's not normally so busy." She snatched a pair of scissors from a workbench along the wall and turned back to face Matt. "Seeley offered to stay, but I sent her home. That was before I realized how difficult it would be to get out of *this* thing."

She pointed the scissors at the corset, her cheeks blushing with heat as Matt's eyes followed the movement.

"If you give me a second," Erica explained, "I'll cut myself out and finish getting changed." She gestured again to the corset and then to the crimson fabric of the curtain which shielded the changing area.

As she turned to do just that, Matt planted his large hand on her shoulder, halting her retreat, forcing her to glance back.

"You shouldn't have to destroy something so lovely," Matt told her. "Maybe I could help you unlace it?"

The giggle that left Erica's lips was a little too high-pitched for her liking. She swallowed deeply, trying to consume the huge, thick ball of nerves that had clumped itself at the back of her throat. "That's a pick-up line I haven't heard before."

Matt's kind eyes widened innocently, and he snatched his hand from her arm. "Sorry, I really hadn't meant it that way." He shook his head as though mentally correcting his thoughts. "You're just so stunning. I mean, it is. I'd just hoped I could save it, stop you attacking it with the scissors by offering to help you out of it."

As he scrambled to find the right words, Erica laughed. "So basically, you're offering to help me out of my underwear?"

Matt's breath caught, and his handsome, angular cheekbones warmed with obvious embarrassment. "Well—" his attention dropped to her ample cleavage as though immediately realizing her nudity beneath the troublesome piece of clothing. "I guess, if you put it that way … sort of."

When she laughed again, he joined her.

"Look, I can't think of anything I want more at this moment than to be rid of this thing, so if you want to take a shot at untying the mess I've made, be my guest." Erica handed him the scissors.

Matt smirked at her, his eyes sparkling with amusement. "We won't be needing these," he told her, placing them safely on a nearby table.

Her gaze darkened in challenge, and she turned her back on him.

Ignoring the ache deep in her gut, the pleasurable throb

that seemed to be mounting as each millisecond passed, Erica inhaled deeply and waited for him to begin. She felt his touch through the silky fabric, light at first, before a gentle tugging began. The soft slap of a rogue lace hitting her shoulder blade, sliding down her back, had goosebumps bubbling over her skin, pricking her sensitive nipples tighter. She could feel the warmth of his body so near to hers, could smell the spicy heat of his skin, could hear his breathing, ragged like hers as he tried desperately to focus on his task.

The gentle tugging continued, her body suddenly pulled back toward his, the movement out of her control before the tightness of his hold released her once more. Again and again he pulled her to him, her body inching closer to his each time and then his grip would loosen. It seemed so sensual, the thrusting movement, back and forth, and yet, he hadn't even touched her, not skin to skin. His fingers stuck chastely to their innocent task, untying the lace, loosening the bind of the boned corset without dithering.

Erica struggled against the heady lust that was intoxicating her. As the material of the corset gaped slightly, she held it up over her breasts, trying to ensure she remained modest even though all of her instincts were willing her not to. Matt pulled her toward him one final time and then the corset hung around her, loose enough that, had she not been holding onto it, it would surely have dropped over her hips.

"That should do it." Matt's voice was coarse, croaky, even though it held a lilt of triumph.

Erica sighed loudly, knowing the relief she felt was evident in the noise. She was so grateful to finally be on the verge of freedom from the constrictive piece of clothing and of the strangely intimate interaction. It wasn't as though she hadn't enjoyed the encounter, it was because she'd relished it too much that she'd been worried. Her willpower, although minimal to begin with, had all but completely dissolved throughout the ordeal, and, had Matt not then announced the completion of his task, she might have let her desire override sense.

"Thanks." She risked a glimpse over her shoulder at him. "Believe it or not, I was starting to feel claustrophobic."

Matt released a tense chuckle. "Understandably." He took a step back from her, moving his hand to the edge of the crimson curtain beside them. "I'll wait for you to get changed."

Again, she felt a surge of relief, but this time it was mixed with a sharp twinge of disappointment, a painful wrenching in her heart, and much deeper, that held her frozen for an instant.

"Of course." The words left her lips automatically as she urged herself to turn, to face him, smiling her appreciation. But the smile wouldn't come.

Erica stared at him, into those captivating gold-flecked irises, clasping the loosened cream corset to her chest, as her inner turmoil intensified. Matt's gentle eyes changed, heating under her stare, growing lustful, passionate, and desperate.

"Could you—" The words slipped out. She hadn't meant them to.

Her gaze left his, glancing at where his hand still held the curtain ajar, before returning. She watched him do the same, but when his eyes met hers, his desirous expression became remorseful.

"Sorry." He moved the crimson fabric toward her, cutting a barrier between them.

She released her tight hold on the corset and covered his hand with her own, stopping his movement.

"No." She shook her head.

Electricity buzzed beneath her fingertips, through his hand to hers. Instinctively, her fingers entangled with his, causing him to release the curtain.

"Could you come closer?"

Matt's eyes widened in surprise. Erica used her hold to

pull him forward, and he stumbled toward her, still uncertain.

"Erica?"

She raised his hand to her cheek, placing it against the softness of her skin, savoring in its warmth, its size and strength as it cupped her face, his thumb caressing a neat line over her cheekbone. The hint of concern in Matt's eyes faded quickly, his body relaxing before an eager confidence, a sensual hunger consumed him.

"I can't believe I hardly know you." He groaned. "It feels like you've always been mine."

In a different situation, with another person, those words would have shocked her, had her laughing in his face—or slapping it—but, in this case, they felt so unequivocally true. She'd had the same unnerving feeling since meeting him, that same intuition that he belonged with her.

Erica closed the short distance between them, pressing her body to Matt's, before slipping both hands around the back of his neck.

"I'll be yours," she told him, "for tonight."

Something in his eyes ignited, and he lowered his head, his soft mouth capturing hers, molding, consuming, growing ardent as he used his free hand to clutch her against him. She drowned in the deliciousness of him, the honeyed taste of his mouth, the fervent caress of his tongue as it danced with hers. She inhaled him, the scent of skin, soap, and man, as her fingers raked through the thickness of his dark brown hair.

He slid his hand from her waist over the curve of her bottom, and Erica heard herself moan as he pressed her body against him. The size of him had her body yearning, hot moisture pooling at the delta of her thighs, dampening her panties. He was already hard but trapped beneath the smooth fabric of his black work slacks. Erica dropped her hands from his hair and neck, then reached for his belt, her fingers nimble as she unclasped it.

The corset slipped down with the movement, sinking below the tight tips of her nipples, letting them scrape sensitively over the gray material of Matt's shirt. The sensation rocketed through her, pulling at something deep in her groin, sending little fireworks of ecstasy throughout her body. She clutched at his hips, her head falling back as his hot kisses trailed a line of fire down her throat, and she moaned.

The heavenly throbbing at her core ached for him, wanting him to fill her. Matt moved his hand to the fullness of her breast, kneading, stroking, while using his thumb to toy with her pert nipple. With his other hand on her bare back, he held her to him as his lips found their way over her collarbone down to the curvaceous mound of her other breast. He used his teeth to nip at her, his tongue to lick over the plump skin, then took the nipple into his mouth and suckled on it. He swirled his crafty tongue as she arched her chest toward him.

Erica cried out, then bit her lower lip in pleasurable agony. She needed him now. She drew her hand to his face, lifting it to hers, her lips seizing his in a devouring kiss as she continued in her mission to free him of his trousers. Matt skimmed his hands down her body, pushing the corset over her hips, taking the denim shorts with it, then her lace panties. He slid them lower until they fell to the floor. Erica stepped free of them, kicking them aside, her mouth roaming from his down to the curve of his neck as she finally unzipped his slacks.

The warmth of his hands left her while he ripped at his own shirt, buttons popping free of their stitching as he hurried to drag it from his body. As the garment fell to the floor, Matt reached into the back of his trouser and snatched out his wallet before Erica could slip the waistband down his hips. Once he freed a foil packet from a side pocket inside the leather pouch, he tossed the wallet to the floor.

Matt returned his mouth to hers, eating hungrily at her

lips, his tongue stroking her senseless as he helped her tug his black slacks and blue boxers from his hips to the floor, kicking his shoes off as he did so. He pulled her to him again, skin against skin, arms clasping around her, the foil packet between his fingers cool on her heated flesh. Erica moaned into his mouth as she felt the thickness of him stroke her belly, digging into her, sending tingles of desire to burst deep inside of her.

Then Matt was urging her backward, walking with her, their bodies entwined until her back hit the classroom wall. His lips left hers, teeth tearing at the corner of the foil packet, while the weight of his body held her snug and steady against the cool, smooth surface. Matt slipped his hand between them, purposely caressing a sensitive path down her body before strapping the protection over himself. Then used his fingers to touch her deeper, stroking and opening, slipping inside of her, into the moist depths until she was on her tippy-toes, grinding against his hand. Soft moans left her throat as he found her sweet spot and kissed her throat, using his teeth to nip at her velvet skin.

Just as she believed she might shatter, fracturing into an explosion of ecstasy and light, he slipped his fingers free of her, grabbing her bottom and lifting her. Erica wrapped her legs around Matt's waist, fitting naturally, perfectly around him as he lowered her slowly, sliding into her, inch by inch.

The size of him was overwhelming as she stretched to accommodate him, but it felt so good, so right, she wanted more of him. He buried himself deep inside of her until she felt a sated fullness, a tantalizing wholeness that made her want to keep him there, inside of her always. He flicked his tongue out to lick along her jaw, kissing her chin, her cheek, her lips. She moaned partly in protest, partly in craving, as he pulled out of her, his body still pressing her against the wall as he began a rhythm, thrusting in and out, slowly at first and then intensifying.

His ragged breathing became a groan, and he nipped at her lower lip. Her breasts grazed him, her nipples skimming the smattering of dark hair on his muscular chest as he drove into her. She felt her climax building, the painful yet heavenly tingling consuming her, the sparks of sensation spreading through her as her toes curled. She clenched her thighs around him, and her breath came in short, sharp gasps. The feeling of him filling her was addictive, the intensity of their rhythm, his rock-hard body rubbing against the softness of hers was exhilarating. She couldn't get enough of him, didn't want him to stop, but she couldn't contain the pleasure anymore.

As he thrust into her again, she cried out, her body clenching around his, her head swimming, elated thoughts swirling. Through the intense explosions of euphoria making her quiver and the blissful warmth enchanting her core, she heard Matt gasp, felt him shudder as he lost himself to his own powerful climax.

CHAPTER 11

Electronic music wafted around Erica. It was eerie at first, not quite harmonious with her hazy surroundings. She was in the bathtub, Matt's body wrapped around hers, but the weight of his embrace was weakening, and a cloudiness, like a building fog, was coming between them. Her lashes fluttered as the music grew louder, piercing through the misty dream scene, and she opened her eyes.

Her cell phone was buzzing, doing a vibrating dance on top of a workbench beside a pair of scissors. Upbeat electronic tune, something she'd chosen from the preexisting tunes already on the device, played melodically as it increased in volume. Startled, Erica shot upright, pulling free of Matt's embrace from where they'd been sleeping together, snuggling on the small life drawing stage. She clutched the crimson fabric curled around them to her bare chest, quickly remembering how they'd torn the curtain free of its hooks during an even more amorous round two. Blush heated her face at the memory of the night's events as she admired Matt's sleeping form, his handsome face so peaceful that it lured her, urging her to touch him, to kiss him.

Suddenly, the loud pulsing of the music ceased, making

the abrupt silence seem deafening. Erica's heartbeat sped in response, fear overwhelming her as she tried to gather her wits about her.

It was Saturday, she was sure of that. It was Saturday, and she had her pastels class at ten.

Crap!

She bent her head then lifted it, moving around in an effort to view the clock on the far wall above the service counter in the storefront. It was just after nine.

Sighing, she relaxed a little, feeling her rapid heartbeat, which had neared the verge of a panic attack, finally begin to slow. But there were other things to worry about—like the naked man sleeping beside her, the fact that she hadn't cleaned up the classroom, the phone call that had woken her, her class at ten. Oh, and maybe the fact that she'd slept with said naked man beside her, numerous times. The man she supposedly didn't want a relationship with, while all the other women in town were totally keen for one. The man she now had to kick out, so she could clean up.

Surely a "Thanks for the wham, bam, but it's never going to happen again, man," would be enough explanation, wouldn't it? Even if parts of her didn't agree with it, parts too licentious or romantically-inclined to want to let him go, it was the right thing to do, wasn't it? She'd sworn off men, was supposed to be focusing on her career, on herself, it wouldn't be fair to him to lead him on. Right?

Erica dropped her head in her hands.

Lead him on? If last night wasn't the most encouragement she'd ever shown a man in her life, she wasn't sure what else would top it. Of course, she had said "for tonight" before they'd started anything, that she'd be his for this one-time event, but her actions during the course of the night may have suggested otherwise.

She was almost certain she'd said some things in the heat of the moment, while her brain was completely befuddled with lust, which seemed terribly embarrassing in hindsight.

I can't get enough of you.

I love the way you feel inside of me.

Please do that to me every night for the rest of my life.

Erica cringed, a guttural groan of humiliation slipping through her lips.

The sound of movement, a sudden shifting on the stage-slash-makeshift bed and a rustling of fabric, had her lifting her head free of her hands.

Matt lay on his back, his hands under his head, biceps bulging as he gazed up at her sleepily.

"Morning." His voice was cheerful but husky with drowsiness.

Erica found herself smiling down at him, the optimist inside of her basking in the adoration evident in his eyes. Her heart filled her chest, swelling larger with warm contentment.

"You look quite pleased with yourself."

He released a rumbling, throaty chuckle and moved a hand from beneath his head to rest on the soft, bare skin of her hip. He caressed her affectionately, habitually, as though the motion was so familiar, so comfortable to him.

"I've got a lot to be pleased about," he agreed as he used his fingers to draw enticing circles on her flesh.

The electricity that radiated from him, the tingling sensation humming from his fingertips into her skin, sparked an intense need she'd hoped she'd already sated. How could her body still want him? She was tender, pleasingly so, all over, her muscles tired after having been stretched and strained during the vigorous activities of the past evening. What she really needed was a long hot shower, maybe a few more hours of sleep in her own bed, not another roll in the sheets with the sexiest man on the planet.

"I don't know what you're talking about." The playful quip rolled off her tongue instinctively.

She bent closer to him, knowing she had to get up, get

away if she wanted any chance of organizing the room in time for the impending pastels class. He smoothed his hand up her side, causing goosebumps to follow the trail, and pricking her already alert nipples tighter. Erica dipped her face to his, enjoying Matt's eager response, his eyes darkening, his tongue sneaking out to wet his lips as she reached a hand across his solid chest. Her lips brushed his, tickling over the softness of his mouth as she grasped his corner of the crimson curtain.

Before he had a chance to realize her gambit, she yanked the material from him and jumped to her feet, wrapping the silky fabric around herself and leaving him cold, fully naked, and standing to attention. Erica grinned down at him triumphantly, unable to help herself from momentarily admiring his happy package. The sight of him, completely naked and ready for her, tugged pleasurably at her insides, making her wish they had more time together.

Matt quirked a dark eyebrow. "You know, that won't protect you for long." He gestured to the curtain now securing her modesty.

"Sorry, but your night's over, lover boy, and I've got a job to do."

Concern had him sitting up, perching himself on his elbows. "You have a class?" He peered around the room as though taking in the mess left over from the life drawing lesson.

She nodded, wondering if he'd purposely chosen not to react to the first part of her statement. "At ten."

Matt climbed to his feet and stepped toward her. "How much time do we have?"

She inched away from him. "Not enough time to do anything more than dress and clean."

"Is that a challenge?"

She felt her stomach swirl nauseously. How was she going to explain to him that this couldn't continue? He needed to know he was better off finding someone else, being with someone who could give him the relationship he desired. But he looked so exuberant, so pleased, and a part of her felt the same.

An ache in her chest grew as though something inside was begging her to give him a chance. It was like her subconscious was doing its best to convince her that her man-free period had reached its natural conclusion and that maybe this guy was worth taking the risk for. But was he? And could she? Her instincts had been wrong before—too many times to forget.

Matt's jovial humor dissipated as he assessed her features. "What's wrong, Erica?" He hurried over to her, hugging his arms around her before she could escape him.

Erica loved the way his body molded around hers, as though it were made for her. She fit within his embrace so perfectly.

Shaking her head, she stiffened. She was ready to pray for control, pleading to a higher power to remove this outrageous desire, this desperate need she had for him, if she only believed it would help.

"I can't do this," she told him, her voice pained. "I think you're great, Matt, but …" She slid a hand between them, pushing his solid, muscular chest away to gaze up into his compassionate hazel eyes. "I'm not looking for anything serious at the moment."

"I know, Erica. I'm not expecting anything."

She gnawed at her lower lip until it hurt. "You're okay then?"

He nodded slowly, rubbing his nose along hers before placing a kiss on its tip. "I'm okay."

Breathing out a sigh, she relaxed in his arms.

Unexpectedly, Matt's mouth covered hers, kissing, tasting, nibbling briefly before he then pulled away again. Erica swooned, having been caught off guard by the sensuous attack, her body thrumming with scrumptious sensitivity, wanting him to continue, to place those kisses elsewhere, everywhere.

"What was that for?" Her voice was raspy with lust.

His satisfied grin widened. "I told you I'm not expecting anything, but that doesn't mean I'm not hoping to change your mind."

CHAPTER 12

"What? Couldn't you decide on an outfit? Or are you about to tell me you had to wait twenty minutes for a family of ducks to cross the road?

Matt ignored Nate's mocking and stepped over the threshold into the entryway.

"Not that I should have to explain anything to you, my persnickety friend," Matt teased as Nate closed the door behind him, "because tardiness to a last-minute dinner is not punishable by death—no matter what you might think, but ... I couldn't find my house keys."

Nate offered Matt a dismissive hand gesture and led the way farther inside the modern, sparsely-decorated bungalow. "You always stick them in that thing, the porcelain tray in the kitchen. Even I know that."

Matt shrugged, then slid his hands over the hem of his black polo shirt and into the pockets of his blue jeans. "Well, they weren't there. I found them on the bedside table. I must've been a bit distracted when I got home yesterday."

Nate glanced over his shoulder suspiciously as they entered the spacious living room. "What happened yesterday?"

"Shouldn't I be asking you that question? You're the one who ended up with three women hanging off your every word … and appendage on Friday night."

Nate laughed and took a seat on the wide black leather sofa, his creased checkered shirt and beige chinos crinkling even more with the movement. He'd already lined up a few bottles of beer and prepared an arrangement of finger food on the coffee table in front of them. Even though Matt had been invited over to watch the new action flick Nate had been raving about for weeks, Sunday night football was already playing vibrantly, but quietly, on the big screen television on the wall.

"Four women." Nate held up four fingers as Matt sat beside him. "After you did a runner, Tonya decided I was worth the competition and did her best to scare off the twins, but I think that only succeeded in riling Nicolette even more." He fired a confident wink Matt's way. "I'm grateful for my four though. I found out we were lucky to have the assortment we had. Apparently, a lot of ladies who'd planned to attend had ended up with food poisoning from some lingerie party and had to organize others to go in their stead."

Matt frowned. "Erica said something similar about the model she'd organized." He snatched a corn chip from the bowl nearest him, crunching and devouring it loudly. "So, did you happen to choose a favorite at the end of the night?"

Nate grinned slyly and took a sip of his beer. "I made out with Chloe in the men's, but sadly, I went home alone."

"Yeah, because if you'd made a poor choice, there's all likelihood you would've ended up with a black eye."

Nate picked a bottle of beer off the table and handed it to Matt. He clinked the necks together in a non-verbal cheers and then narrowed his gaze. "So, what happened yesterday?"

Matt took a long drink from the bottle. "I really

thought I'd thrown you off track."

"Well, you didn't, so fess up. I'm thinking you had a better time the other night than you expected."

Matt hated it, but he couldn't help himself—he smiled. He just knew it was one of those elatedly happy smiles. A smile which told way too much, giving mountains of information away to nosy, single-minded friends.

He'd been thinking about his night with Erica for the whole weekend. Even their morning together had been exhilarating. He just loved spending time with her, loved touching her, talking to her. Even though it was painfully obvious that she'd been hoping the one-night-stand she'd agreed to would stay just that, he was going to do everything in his power to make sure their time together continued.

What he had with Erica was something very special, something most other people only ever dreamed of. They fit so well together, so impeccably, their natural chemistry was so intense it already had him craving her, her body, her company. Why couldn't she sense that? Or if she could, why was she fighting it? Her desire to end things and remain friends completely confused him. The sex together had been mind-blowing, and yet, all she wanted from him was a platonic friendship.

Matt had warned her that he'd be trying to change her mind, but he'd done his best not to push the subject as he'd helped her tidy up for her Saturday morning class. He'd even been polite, kissing her on the cheek when he'd said his good-byes, ignoring his instincts to pull her into his arms and kiss her until she melted against him. Yet now, he was starting to regret all of that. After she'd warily agreed to give him her phone number—now they were *friends*—he'd texted her more times than he'd like to admit, more times in the past thirty-three hours than a grown man should've felt obliged to.

He took another sip of his beer as the uneasiness, the slight queasiness of regret, washed over him.

"This distracted look you've got on is not going to throw me, buddy." Nate waved a hand in front of Matt's face. "I'm waiting for your answer, and it better be a good one. What happened to you yesterday?"

Matt tried to ignore the wariness sitting heavily in his stomach. "I came home from Unique Art Boutique, that's all."

Nate's auburn brows furrowed. "You came home," he parroted back, clearly digesting the words, "from Unique Art Boutique."

Matt nodded and drank another gulp of beer.

"You came … home?"

"That wasn't supposed to be a brain-teaser," Matt growled.

Nate's gaze flicked back to him, and his expression cleared in delight. "You came home!"

Excitement buzzed from Nate's body, making Matt cringe.

"We've established that," he told Nate sharply.

"You know when I asked you to talk to her, to try to convince her to start up a singles class to help us meet women, I never expected you to go the extra mile to seal the deal."

"Firstly," Matt growled, holding up his index finger to make a point, "that singles night class was supposed to help *you* meet women, not me, and secondly, I haven't had a chance to ask her yet."

"Laying the groundwork before you ask for the favor, huh? Smart move."

Matt glowered at him. "If you don't want me to leave before the movie has even started then stop acting like a douchebag."

"Not going to kiss and tell, hey? Oh well, at least I know you got some, and Lord, you needed it." Nate lifted the beer bottle to his lips.

"The douchebag level is rising," Matt warned.

Nate finished the drink in a long gulp. As his gaze met

Matt's again, his smirk was strangely unsettling.

"I'm not asking for intimate details." Nate held up a hand, palm facing Matt as though in defense. "I'm serious, mate. But, I can clearly see something's bothering you. Maybe it would help to get it off your chest."

Matt knew what Nate was doing. He was being nice and supportive—a rare occurrence for him—and it was likely he was doing so solely to achieve his goal: to get Matt to reveal more of his night with Erica than he needed to.

Still, Matt did need this, he needed someone to talk to, if only to put his mind at ease. He knew he shouldn't be stressing, so concerned about what Erica thought of him, whether she would ever give in and let their relationship begin. But, he couldn't stop his mind from getting distracted by possibilities—both the good and the bad. What if he could never convince her they deserved to have a relationship together, deserved to see where it might lead them? Or what if he'd ruined everything by hounding her with texts without waiting for her to reply? Or was that an even worse thing—her lack of reply? Was that a sign he'd been too pushy and had, in fact, already pushed her away?

He slumped back into the leather sofa. "Okay. You're probably the worst person to ask, but I need to talk to someone about this."

"I'm going to pretend you meant to say *best* instead of worst," Nate quipped. "Now, what's your dilemma? Have you changed your mind now the challenge is over and you've scored? Or has she become a stage-five clinger and you can't shake her off?"

"You're entering douchebag territory again," Matt groaned. "More the last part and more me."

"What do you mean?"

"I'm worried I'm the stage-five clinger and she's trying to shake me free."

Nate's jaw fell. "No." The word rang with disbelief. "Buddy," he drawled, stretching out the syllables. "What's she done to you?"

"Erica told me she's not looking for anything serious, that she doesn't want a relationship, but I've never wanted anything more. So, how the hell do I convince her to give me a shot?"

Nate held up a hand to stop him. "Wait a minute. She's willing to keep screwing you without requiring a commitment, and you want to go and stuff that up?" His eyes were wide as he clasped a hand over his mouth. "There really *is* something wrong with you."

"That's not what I said."

Matt had to wonder if Nate might be right. Was there really something wrong with him? Not in the sense his friend was implying, but something that might be keeping Erica away? A personality trait, a physical characteristic, something he'd said or done? Besides texting her ten times without waiting for a reply.

"So, she won't sleep with you?"

Matt sighed. "Not exactly. She said she wanted us to be friends, but I want the whole package—the sex, the relationship, the love. I just want *her*."

"*Friends*." Nate spat out the word as though it had a bad taste, before placing his empty beer on the coffee table beside him and grabbing a new bottle. "That's the kiss of death, buddy."

Matt nodded in agreement as he rubbed his fingers over his creased brow.

"Guess we can scratch her off our potential cupcake maker list?"

"This is serious, Nate. I need a game plan."

Nate took a drink of his fresh beer and then tapped his fingers on the belly of the bottle. "Well, she clearly likes you enough to sleep with you, so why don't you use the man-whoring abilities I've taught you to try to seduce some feelings into her?"

"Figures your suggestion would involve sex."

"Hey, I'm trying to help you here." After watching the

television for an instant, Nate clicked his fingers. "I've got it. Why don't you talk to Seeley? She could give you some insight into what Erica's looking for."

Matt eyed the game on the big screen before glancing back at Nate. "Not sure what it was about big, brutish football players that made you think of Seeley—"

"Isn't it obvious?"

Matt ignored him. "But, that's actually not a bad idea. At least Seeley could tell me if I'm doing anything wrong."

"See, told you I'm good with the romantic advice."

Normally, Matt would never have concurred with that statement, but in this specific case, his friend's suggestion offered him a next step, progress of some sort. It seemed obvious now, that when it came to winning Erica's heart, he was going to need some help.

CHAPTER 13

In the depths of her paisley-patterned shoulder bag, Erica could feel her mobile phone vibrating. The sensation rumbled through the fabric against her jean-clad hip like a weak intermittent massage. She wasn't game to check it, not again. That was one of the reasons she'd turned it to silent.

Ever since Saturday morning she'd been receiving text messages from Matt, and calls from an unknown number. Although the calls were likely related to last Friday's life drawing class, when she'd managed to answer a couple, she hadn't been able to keep the connection. There would be silence for a long moment as she spoke into the receiver, and then the call would cut dead. It wasn't so unusual, really. There were plenty of women from Friday's class who lived on acreage a fair distance from town where mobile coverage could be dicey. Erica hoped whoever it was would give up the futile effort and try the landline.

The buzzing vibrations finally stopped as she neared Forrest's Organics, the fresh produce store across the road from the Montville Information Centre. Erica sighed deeply, noticing for the first time how tired and anxious the repetitive calls were making her feel. If anything, they were just annoying. She knew she couldn't do anything about them, because she didn't know who the caller was. Without that knowledge, she couldn't contact the person in a different way or stop the incessant ringing.

Yet, she couldn't say the same thing about Matt's texts. They didn't stress her out in quite the same way. In fact, a warmth blossomed through her, making her tingle with excitement every time she noticed a message from him. Problem was, she was smart enough to recognize that as a bad sign and so, had done her best to ignore them, and him, in the hopes of ridding herself of the feelings she feared she'd already developed.

She'd been terrible, not getting back to him. They were supposed to be friends now after all, but this was about emotional survival. If she had to keep her distance from him, ignore all attempts at communication to ensure her heart was protected, then so be it. She was going to be smart about romance this time and not get herself involved in it—that was the plan. At least Monday was down, she'd survived the day without giving in to any silly inclinations to respond. If she just took it day by day she'd be fine. *Right?*

As the automatic door slid open invitingly, Erica strode into the cool air-conditioned store, her eyes quickly adjusting from the fading light of dusk outside to the bright fluorescents. She glanced from the racks of fresh fruit and vegetables, past the shelves of packaged foodstuffs, around the odd customer, before looking over at the counter. Lauren stood behind it dressed in a green T-shirt with the store's logo on the breast. Her thumbs tapped rhythmically on the screen of her mobile phone before she finally looked up. When she noticed Erica heading over, her cheeks reddened slightly, and she put down the device.

"Bad habit." Lauren nodded toward the back of the store. "Joe, the owner, he lets me keep it close in case of emergencies."

"I understand," Erica told her. "It's so tempting when you have the whole Internet at your fingertips."

Lauren gave her a nod. "So, is there something I can help you with?"

"Actually, I wanted to give some organic chocolate a go. Maybe try some of that wine you suggested, see how it compares."

"Sure thing." Lauren rounded the counter and led Erica deeper into the building. "I think the dark chocolate's the best." She pointed at a couple of blocks on the shelf in front of them.

Erica immediately noticed that there was a size difference, block-wise. Why was it healthier things always came in smaller packages?

"As for the wine," Lauren continued, leading her away from their version of a confectionary aisle to the farthest end of the room, "I'm guessing you were after alcoholic, but were you wanting a red or white?"

Erica scanned the lineup of bottles of the shelf in front of her. She hadn't realized organic wine was so popular. "One of each maybe. Do you have any suggestions?"

"Do I?" She pulled a black bottle decorated with a blue label and a couple of gold medal stickers off the top shelf. "Samber Creek cabernet merlot is a staff favorite here, and"—she passed the bottle to Erica before scanning the shelves again—"the Butterfly Canyon pinot grigio is my go-to for white." She grabbed a green bottle from the middle shelf and handed it over, swapping out the cabernet merlot in Erica's grasp for the new suggestion.

Erica turned the cool glass of the weighty bottle over in her hands as she considered the options. With a nod, she handed the pinot grigio back to Lauren. "Great. I'll get both."

"I'll take them back to the counter while you browse the chocolate, shall I?"

"Thanks."

As Lauren hurried away, Erica called out to stop her.

"I've been meaning to ask you how your painting is coming along. Have you started on that large canvas yet?"

Lauren turned back to her abruptly, a flicker of something unsettled in her eyes. Was it nervousness? Maybe worry? Erica hadn't meant to pry.

"It's coming along. Slowly. I need it to be perfect."

"I'm sure it will be." Erica understood the desire every artist had to precisely replicate the image in their head. "I'd love to display it in the gallery when you're finished." She saw something flash across Lauren's face—annoyance maybe, more likely fear—and she immediately regretted the suggestion. "Only if you're interested, of course."

"Thanks." Lauren's reply was curt. "But I have something else in mind for it."

Erica nodded several times. "Okay."

Lauren gave her a sharpish smile, a baring of teeth, and turned away.

Irritated with herself for upsetting the younger woman, Erica closed her eyes for a moment before heading back to the chocolate aisle. As she weighed her options, literally, with a block in each hand, the light *click* and quiet *whoosh* of the automatic door had her glancing upward. With a wave in Lauren's direction, Diana—still dressed in the burgundy and beige uniform of the Montville Information Center—made her way to the counter, a broad grin stretching her red lipstick-covered lips. Erica watched the friends greet each other cheerfully and then froze as Diana's gaze snapped to hers. Having been caught in her stare, Erica waved the block of chocolate in her right hand at them and quickly turned back to her dessert choices as the conversation at the counter went from a jubilant pitch to a hushed murmur.

Great, now I feel like the third wheel, Erica mused.

Not wanting to interrupt them further, and figuring this was as good a chance as any to peruse more of the store, Erica moved down the aisle and into the next. The familiar *click*, then *whoosh* of the front door tried to trick her into looking up again, but she knew better this time.

"Lauren, how are you doing, love?"

Erica slapped a hand over her face as she recognized Jocelyn's bright, chirpy tones. She was bound to be in for a scolding for one reason or another if the older woman caught sight of her.

Drifting inconspicuously toward the farthest corner of the shop, Erica continued to listen to what she could hear of the conversation at the counter.

"How's your mother, Diana? Getting over that flu?"

"Yes, Ms. Weaver. She's doing much better."

"Glad to hear it. You tell her I hope to see her at church this Sunday."

"Will do."

Erica could hear the pad of footsteps on the concrete floor, and soundlessly prayed they'd head in the opposite direction.

"If you're looking for Erica," Lauren offered, "she was headed toward the pickled vegetables."

Erica's blood went cold, and she cursed silently. Lauren might have thought she was helping, but she'd inadvertently earned herself a black cross against her name in Erica's metaphorical book.

"Really?" Jocelyn sounded exuberant and the footsteps quickened.

Seeing no point in delaying the inevitable, Erica made her way to the end of the aisle, toward her pursuer. "Jocelyn," she crooned, surprising the older woman.

"Erica, dear, I didn't know you were shopping organic these days." As she observed the two blocks of chocolate in Erica's hands, she frowned. "Chocolate is not a meal, sweetheart."

"The wine is ready to go when you are." Lauren piped up from the counter.

Erica swallowed deeply and mentally added a second black cross against the considerate young woman's name.

Jocelyn squinted over at the countertop to where two

tall bottles poked above the serrated edge of the brown paper bag. Then her criticizing gaze, having become even more disapproving, returned to Erica's again.

"I hope you're not planning to drink both of those tonight, young lady."

Erica shrugged. "They're my two serves of fruit for the day."

When Jocelyn's jaw dropped in alarm, Erica rolled her eyes and placed a calming hand on the ginger-haired woman's shoulder. "I'm kidding, Jocelyn. Don't give yourself a coronary."

Though the way Erica was feeling, two bottles of wine might just settle her mood nicely.

Jocelyn released a couple of short huffs of laughter. "Of course, dear."

When Erica saw Jocelyn's gaze roam past her paint-stained clothes and down to the bare scab on her injured knee, she knew it was time to make her exit.

"Well, I'll see you at class tomorrow then." She ducked past Jocelyn and headed for the counter.

"Have you been for a check-up?" Jocelyn called after her. "You need to make sure the wound is healing properly."

"It's healing fine," Erica retorted over her shoulder as she finally reached the counter.

Diana moved to the side, still watching the whole debacle, just as the front door *swooshed* quietly open and Matt strode in.

His gaze lifted, meeting Erica's—as though he only had eyes for her—and then a grin, wide, triumphant, and sultry as hell set his handsome features alight. "Fancy seeing you here."

Erica's mouth opened, but the expletives she'd meant to say remained noiseless curses in her head.

"What perfect timing, Dr. Garrick," Jocelyn beamed as she came up beside Erica. "Would you have a moment to check Erica over? You know what she's like with doctors."

When Jocelyn laughed at her expense, Erica scowled.

"I'm fine. My knee's all but completely healed. You don't have to waste your time on me, Dr. Garrick."

His gaze narrowed at her words, a smirk pulling at his lips as though he were eager to accept the challenge. "It's no trouble at all, Miss Townsend."

When she glowered at him, his smile grew bigger.

"That'll be thirty-two fifty total, if you're wanting to take both blocks, as well."

Startled by Lauren's sharpness, Erica glanced across the countertop at the younger woman who was looking anxiously from the chocolates in Erica's hands and over to where Matt was standing in front of the door. Did she think Erica was intending to walk out without paying for them? Or perhaps Lauren was just being helpful again?

"Thanks, Lauren." Erica dug around in her shoulder bag for her wallet. "And thank you for your help with everything, too."

As Erica handed over the money, the younger woman smiled and then passed back a few coins in change.

"Let me know what you think of the wine."

"Will do." While Erica dropped the blocks of chocolate into her brown paper bag, she heard Diana speak up behind her.

"Hi Matt, it's lovely to see you again."

"You too, Diana." He sounded distracted.

"Are you going to attend the life drawing class this Friday?"

Fighting the urge to roll her eyes, Erica reached for the shopping bag. As she prepared to pick up the heavy parcel and make a quick exit, Matt intervened, snatching up her groceries and linking his muscular arm through hers.

Stupefied into silence, Erica watched as he threw an answer over his shoulder at Diana.

"If Erica will have me." Then he aimed a smile at Jocelyn, who'd already raised a hand as though to halt them. "No need to worry, Ms. Weaver, I'll be sure to check her out thoroughly." Matt's grin remained as he offered all three women a blanket good-bye, then dragged Erica through the open doorway.

CHAPTER 14

They were almost to the parking lot across the street when Erica returned to her senses. She tried to yank her arm free of Matt's, but he wouldn't let her, choosing instead to tighten his grip and link his fingers through hers.

"Where are you taking me? Should I be calling for help? Is this a kidnapping?" Even though she could hear the sarcasm in her tone, the slight shrillness of her voice had her cringing. She hadn't meant for him to know she was a little scared.

Matt beamed smugly. "I'm only being friendly, and as your friend, I wanted to give you a lift home."

"There's no need. I'm parked just up the road."

"Your car will be fine where it is for the night."

Erica surveyed the nearly empty parking lot, taking in the peaceful gloom of the coming night, the deepening shadows and the glow of the streetlights. "It better be," she muttered.

He led her to a tall, black Range Rover. "Don't you want to let me do something nice for you?"

He propped her groceries on the bonnet before searching the side pocket of his black slacks. Drawing out the car key, he pressed a button and the lights of the vehicle flashed, signaling its doors had unlocked.

"I can't decide whether you're being nice or being sneaky, but I'm leaning toward the latter."

He laughed as he opened the passenger side door. Releasing his firm hold on her, Matt ushered her toward the interior, ensuring his broad chest remained between her and any escape route she may have been considering.

She glanced back at him before climbing in. "There's no point in fighting you on any of this, is there?"

He shook his head. "Nope."

Once she'd taken a seat, Matt reached beside her shoulder for the seatbelt, pulling it provocatively close over her body, along the cotton of her yellow blouse, before clipping it into place at her hip.

"Now, you just stay there," he commanded as he shut the door.

Erica glared at his back through the clear windshield as he grabbed the weighty brown paper bag off the bonnet and headed to the driver's side. It annoyed her that her skin had prickled with his close proximity, that tingles had trailed the warmth of his hand, and that a delicious yearning had clenched low in her gut. Of course, he'd smelled good, even his car smelled pleasantly of him— fresh and earthy—and he'd felt good, his body had been so close to hers, their fingers interlaced snugly, but that was no reason for her to go all weak at the knees.

She heard the back door *click*, the rough crinkling of the bag settling on the seat, before it closed and Matt opened the driver's side next to her.

"Interesting choice of purchases," he told her as he took his seat and shut the door. "Wine and chocolate. It's like you were hoping to run into me."

Erica rolled her eyes and stared out the passenger window. "That's wishful thinking on your part."

Again, Matt laughed, and she wondered if there was anything she could say that would be able to dampen his cheerful mood.

Erica hadn't responded to Matt's attempt at small talk on the short drive. She didn't want to encourage him and knew the brief trip would be over quickly since she didn't live that far out of town. She was startled, though, when he took the final turn to pull down her long, heavily-treed driveway, especially considering she'd never told him where she lived. She'd been expecting to offer him directions, but he'd never asked.

She listened to the car's tires *crunch* audibly on the gravel chips. "Okay, who'd you bribe to get this information?"

"So, now you're talking to me again?"

"Don't be a sook. It's only been like five minutes."

His eyebrow rose as they traveled around the final bend and parked in front of her rustic-looking, brown and red brick cottage. The gold blaze of the car's headlights lightening the dark wood of the front door and the wide porch that wrapped around the inviting building. When Matt switched off the engine, then the headlights, only the dim glow of the small security light on the porch remained.

"It's a small town," Matt reminded her. "If Melina hadn't told me, there are plenty of other people I could've asked."

He opened his door as quickly as she did, so she turned back to him.

"Thanks for the lift, but there's absolutely no need for you to get out. I'm strong enough to carry my own groceries inside."

She slammed the door shut before giving him a chance to respond, and made her way around the back of the car. On the other side, she noticed he'd exited anyway and now stood beside the open back door.

He motioned to the brown paper bag still sitting on the seat inside. "All yours." Then his friendly expression glinted with something darker, sneakier. "Maybe you'd like

105

to give me the keys to the front door, so I can open it for you. Might be easier." He crossed his arms over his muscular chest and shrugged casually.

There was no way Erica was falling for that. "You think you're pretty clever, don't you?" She picked up the bag of wine and chocolate before closing the car door.

"Well, I am a doctor."

When she stepped around him, heading toward the couple of stairs up to her porch, she sensed him fall into a step behind her. There was a *click*, the flash of lights from his vehicle, and she quickly realized he'd locked the car. She turned back to him.

"Why did you do that? You're not coming inside."

"I beg to differ," he said, overtaking her and stopping at the front entrance.

Erica just glared at him. "What happened to this only being a lift home?"

He shrugged again, that relaxed, but oh-so-confident movement agitated something in her.

"I feel like you owe me one."

She clenched her jaw. "How do you figure?"

"Don't you know it's impolite to ignore text messages from friends?"

Erica bit the inside of her cheeks to avoid saying something she'd probably regret. It was obvious he knew very well why she might have kept quiet, why she might have chosen to avoid contact with him for a while, hoping things between them might simmer down.

Fighting back a growl, she shoved the bag into his chest and searched her shoulder bag for her house keys.

"I thought you were strong enough to carry your own groceries inside?"

"Do you really think it's a good idea to push your luck right now?"

His satisfied grin irked her, but she ignored it. Keys finally in hand, Erica unlocked the front door and stepped inside, flicking on the lights. When she turned at the threshold, hoping to be sneaky herself and prohibit his entry, she saw she was already too late.

Had the paper bag not been between them, not been pressed from his chest to hers, there would've been nothing to stop their bodies from touching. Just the mental image of it had her nipples standing to attention, her breasts swelling in anticipation, which only infuriated her all the more. With that darn grin of his, which was somewhere between hellishly sexy and goddamn irritating, he pushed against her, stepping beyond the threshold and backing her farther inside. When they were a few strides into the safety of the house, he released her, leaving the groceries in her arms, while he went and locked the front door.

"Are you always this bossy?" She knew it was an unfavorable trait, and yet something about his behavior tonight was arousing her desire.

Matt strode back to her, snatching the bag from her grasp as he lowered his lips close to hers. "I prefer to think of it as domineering and no, I only act this way when it's absolutely necessary." He said the word *absolutely* in the snarky tone she'd used with him when she'd exited the car.

God, she wanted to scream at him. Or maybe she just wanted to kiss him?

Her gaze dropped to his full lips, twisted seductively in challenge, but then they were gone and he'd stepped around her into the large kitchen-slash-dining room to his right.

She followed him inside, switching on the light before waving a hand curtly in his direction when she saw him start to unpack the shopping bag. "Make yourself at home, why don't you?"

"Thanks. Who knew you'd be this hospitable?"

Erica glowered at him, at his teasing smirk, and then made her way next to him. "Give me that wine," she ordered. "What do you want red or white?"

He paused. "Red—if you're keen? That was a quick

change of heart."

She snapped the screw top off the bottle of cabernet merlot before reaching above the sink for some wine glasses. "I just realized that if I'm going to make it through this whole charade you've got going, then I'm going to need a few drinks. At least then I can't be held accountable for my actions."

"It's not a charade," he said, leaning in closer to her.

She purposely ignored him and filled the two large glasses with the fragrant wine.

"Do you want the chocolate in the fridge or left out?"

"Left out." She turned to him, both glasses in hand as she watched him scrunch the bag into a ball.

"Recycling?"

Erica pointed to a nearby cabinet and took a long, satiating sip of wine as Matt threw the brown mass into the second of two bins clearly filled with recyclables. When he straightened, he took his glass from her and held it poised.

"Should we make a toast?"

She swallowed another tasty mouthful. "To what? Attempted kidnapping? Uninvited visitors?"

He laughed. "None of those. I know—to friends." As he clinked his glass against hers, she frowned.

"Some *friend* you are, weaseling your way into my house, into my evening. Don't think you'll be able to do the same with my bed tonight."

Erica's eyes grew wide when she realized what she'd said. She sipped at her wine, feeling her cheeks flush with heat. Where had that come from? She'd barely had enough wine to be able to blame her slip of the tongue on the alcohol.

Matt raised his glass and nodded to her. "Now, that, sounded like an invitation."

When he drank deeply from the aromatic red liquid, Erica thought it seemed more like an acceptance of a challenge rather than the consummation of cheers.

CHAPTER 15

Matt could hear a rhythmic buzzing, like the sound of something vibrating. He looked at the wooden coffee table in front of them, noticing the paisley shoulder bag Erica had left on top of it next to the remnants of a frozen pizza and tossed salad. Erica had told him upon opening a second bottle of wine, that since he'd been the one to interrupt her evening, she'd expected him to organize dinner. At least there had been more in her fridge than he had.

And, he mentally reminded himself, he'd need to go grocery shopping tomorrow to rectify that situation—unless, of course, he decided to just move in with her. The thought had him smiling. The benefits of such a change would be more than just a decent food supply.

"Is that your phone?" Matt fought the urge to kiss the top of Erica's head as he brushed a strand of hair from her face.

She sat up from where she'd made herself comfortable, curled up on the sofa beside him after too many glasses of wine. Reaching for her bag, she pulled the phone free.

"Leave me alone," she growled at the device, slamming it screen down on the wooden tabletop.

"Is that how you respond to everyone who tries to contact you?"

She groaned. The light from the television flickered across her contorted features, making her beautiful face glow before she cuddled back under the weight of his outstretched arm. She pressed her head against his chest, hiding her eyes. "You don't understand." It came out muffled as her lips moved the fabric of his navy button-down, tickling the skin beneath.

"Oh, I think I understand all too well," he joked, trying his best to ignore how other parts of his body responded to the feel of her mouth on him. "Some poor person is trying to get a hold of you—calling, texting—desperate to get in touch with you, to hear your voice, and what do you do? Ignore them and then hurt your poor, innocent phone."

Erica slapped his chest and straightened, shifting free of him. "You always have to be the topic of conversation, don't you?"

Matt bit his lower lip as he tried not to smirk. Erica's long dark hair was mussed from where she'd relaxed in his arms, her cheeks slightly pink, her tongue and mannerisms just slightly loosened from the alcohol. He lost himself in her big, brown eyes.

God, he couldn't believe how incredibly gorgeous she was.

When her eyes narrowed on his and she poked his chest with an accusatory index finger, he returned from his fantasies.

"I'll have you know that I tried to answer this person. I did." She glared at him as though daring him to verbalize any doubt. "But every time I pick up the call it always gets disconnected."

Matt bit back a laugh at her poor excuse. Upon seeing her expression become more serious, he frowned. "Well, that's weird."

She shrugged and flopped back on the sofa cushion

beneath his outstretched arm. "See, I'm not as horrible as you think I am."

He watched her quickly become distracted by the flashing lights of the television before slipping his arm from the top of the sofa and then around her shoulders again. "I could never think you short of wonderful," he told her warmly.

Erica snorted softly and shoved at him, then snuggled closer. "You're full of it, you know that?"

He laughed, pulling her securely against his side as he, too, became distracted by the reality show about ridiculously tiny homes. Seconds passed before he reconsidered their conversation.

"Why don't you just text them?"

"What?"

"This person. The phone calls." He pointed at her phone. "Text them and tell them to email you instead. It might just be that they have a shitty mobile."

He felt her shoulders lift half-heartedly beneath his touch.

"I would if I could, but it's an unknown number."

He shifted so he could gaze more clearly into her eyes. "That's really weird."

"It's probably someone in town with a private number. Could even be a telemarketer? I'm sure it'll stop eventually, or they'll figure out another way to contact me."

"But they've been calling you a lot?"

She must've heard the worry in his voice, because she straightened, turning to him as she nodded. "Since Saturday morning."

"The call that woke you?" From where his hand now rested at her lower back, he caressed her reassuringly.

She nibbled at her lower lip. "Yeah."

He could have been making a dam out of a droplet, but it sounded strange. There was an uneasiness roiling in his gut now, making him remember how he'd felt when he'd found his misplaced house keys. Trepidation shivered over his skin for an instant, but he ignored the unsettling feeling. Erica was more than likely right. It was probable the caller was a local, even someone she knew. Either that or a professional trying to sell her useless insurance or wanting her to change electricity companies.

Erica shifted position, pulling Matt free of his thoughts as her jean-clad knee brushed against the material of his black slacks, along the sensitive skin of his outer thigh, before she rested her shapely leg on the sofa between them. That sinfully sexy smile, the one which stirred his groin—and pierced his heart—with an ache of desire, spread her full lips.

"I'm not falling for it," she told him, her voice low and sensual.

Matt danced his fingers in a rhythmic caress beneath the cotton of her yellow blouse and onto her bare skin, then paused. "Falling for what?"

"You're trying to scare me into letting you stay the night."

He couldn't deny he'd had every intention of convincing her to let him sleep over, even if he had to make do with the sofa, but he'd yet to decide on the approach. Although untrue, it seemed as good an attempt as any.

"Why would I do that?" He continued to tickle the soft skin of her back. "You made it perfectly clear earlier that I had no chance of ending up in bed with you tonight."

She rose a dark eyebrow as she settled a hand on the top of his thigh, drawing patterns over the fabric with her fingertips, sending tingles through his skin to build and clutch low inside of him. His trousers tightened as he felt himself grow with an overwhelming need. He was supposed to have more control than this, more willpower, but he yearned for her, ached for her, it was too painful to hide.

"You've got that right, buddy," Erica murmured to him as she rose up on one knee and swung her other leg across to straddle him. "There's no way I'm letting you in my bed, but if you agree to my terms, maybe we can share the sofa."

Her body melted against him, the satisfying weight of her ass on his lap, the luscious mounds of her plump breasts pressed to his chest, while his heart raced with excitement.

Was this really happening? Part of him feared it was a trick.

She slung her arms around his neck as her mouth dipped slowly to his, and his heart swelled. Matt held her to him, pushing her softness against the firmness of his body before he roamed his hands around every curve. He was so ravenous with anticipation, desperate for the taste of her, that when she hesitated an inch away, he almost growled his displeasure.

"Do you agree?"

He felt her sweet breath touch him as though her lips, feather-light, were there.

Agree? Agree to what? He couldn't think clearly.

"No strings," she purred. "This is *not* a relationship."

He heard her words, but they didn't register.

"Not a relationship." Lost in the perfumed scent of her, the soft touch, he echoed it back as though in agreement, as though he understood, but deep down he knew it was a lie.

His answer appeared to please her, causing those full lips to twist happily before they took the final leap to his. Matt enjoyed the gentleness of her kiss, letting her toy with him, taste him, then it became too much. He cupped her face, locking her to him as his mouth claimed hers, as he relished in the mesmerizing sensation of her tongue dancing with his. He ate at her, savoring her breathless moans as he felt her body grind against his, yearning to be touched, to be stroked deeper.

Matt slid his hand from her face, along the velvet skin of her décolletage and began tugging free the buttons of her blouse. He loved the way each eager gasp of breath drew her closer to him, thrusting her breasts along his chest and hand between them. When the last button gave, he tugged the shirt from her shoulders and tossed it to the floor. He glided his hands up her ribs as he broke their kiss and gazed over her, all dark eyes, tousled hair, and swollen lips. Her exquisite tan glowed beneath the flimsy white lace of her bra. His mouth watered as he imagined kissing her, tasting her everywhere.

He watched Erica lick her lips, her pulse jumping in her throat as he slid his hands higher over the delicate ivory material. He rolled his thumbs over the hard peaks of her nipples as she gasped, her eyes closing as he held her. He molded his fingers around the lushness of her curves then skimmed upward to each bra strap. He slipped them over her shoulders, pulling it until each lacy cup flipped down, popping free to reveal every inch of her perfect breasts. Then a wildness overcame him, a carnal hunger, and he wrapped his arms behind her back, drawing her, lifting her to him until he could nip at that plump flesh.

Matt heard her sigh as her head fell back, felt her stroke fingers up his neck and burrow them into his hair. He nibbled at her supple skin, enjoying the softness of it in his mouth before kissing his way to a pert, rosy nipple, and twirling his tongue around the peak. She moved her hips, grinding her body over his groin, forcing the heat of her harder against him, causing a desperate groan to escape his lips.

He'd been trying to prolong their moment together, taking his time to explore her body, savoring all of her in case she decided to keep her distance from him again come tomorrow, but he was losing the battle. Every second spent had the ache inside him building, the desire inside him burning. He yearned for her as though his body needed her touch to survive, as though his heart pumped just to feel her lips against his one more time.

As he licked the saltiness from her skin and kissed a

trail to her collarbone, he felt her straighten. Matt gazed up into her coffee brown eyes, noticing the way they smoldered darkly, hungrily, as Erica stared deep into his soul.

"I need you," she told him in a throaty moan full of unabashed desire.

It was like a defibrillator to his heart, jolting him with elation, igniting the spark of hope that thrived in his depths. It didn't matter why she'd said it—anticipation, desperation, or something more. She'd said it and meant it, and that made him optimistic that the pull between them, the promise of affection he felt, might be mutual.

If only he could answer her, declare what he knew to be true in his heart, but she wasn't ready to hear it, and he wouldn't risk losing what they already had.

He scooped her up in his arms, shifting her until she lay beneath him on the soft sofa cushions. His rapt gaze bore down into hers while his body and soul thrummed with desire and prickled with the electricity of their deeper connection. As he captured her mouth with his again, he used the passionate embrace, his affectionate kiss, to try to show her what he wished to express in words.

I think I'm falling for you, he longed to tell her. *Let me love you.*

CHAPTER 16

"You should probably know, you've acquired a few enemies in town."

The amusement in Seeley's voice had Erica glancing up from her half-eaten cheeseburger to fire a death stare across the countertop. She'd dropped into the Montville Tavern during her friend's usual Wednesday shift for a quick lunchtime catchup. While she'd hoped for some solidarity and helpful advice, especially after sharing her growing dilemma with Matt, Erica had yet to receive anything useful.

"Did the fact that I found my tire slashed yesterday help you come to this conclusion or was it something else?"

Seeley laughed loudly as she placed a fresh glass of diet cola on the empty coaster beside Erica's plate. "Well, you did leave your car all alone, out in the cold in the middle of town."

"You make it sound like I abandoned a child—and I told you, I didn't have much choice in the matter."

"No. You had other more *interesting* things to do." Seeley winked.

Erica threw a french fry at her, but before it could land

greasily on the fabric of her black tank top, Seeley knocked it away with a swipe of her hand.

"Besides, you told me the mechanic found a nail pierced in the rubber? That's hardly having your tire *slashed* now, is it?"

"*Nails*," Erica corrected. "Three, to be exact, and if you weren't referring to that, then what were you talking about?"

Seeley rested the palms of her hands on the varnished wood of the bar's counter. "I was talking to Tonya last night—" she began.

"Tonya?" The startled exclamation caused Erica to choke briefly on her mouthful of food.

"Yes, Tonya, and she told me a number of girls in town aren't too pleased that you invited Matt to your shop to meet single, *emotionally-available* women, only to waste their time by seducing him yourself." Seeley held up a hand as though to stop Erica from complaining. "Don't blame the messenger. They're Tonya's words, not mine."

Anger flushed Erica's cheeks as frustration tightened her chest. How could people think that? She hadn't meant for any of this to happen, least of all the purely sexual relationship she and Matt had stumbled into.

"Is that what you think, Seels?"

Seeley lifted her hands from the bar, holding the palms up as though in surrender. "Hey, I've always been on Team Erica—or Team Sexcapades. All I care about is that you're happy and getting some."

Erica rolled her eyes. At least there was the solidarity she'd been hoping for. She stared down at her half-eaten meal and toyed with a french fry before looking at Seeley.

"Do you think that's why they slashed my tire?"

Seeley crossed her arms and shook her head. "I'm not sure anyone actually damaged your tire, but I have a feeling you're going to get ghosted by a lot of the younger women in Montville until this mess is resolved."

"What do you mean? Getting the silent treatment? Or

less business? Or should I be worried someone might bitch-slap me in the middle of Main Street?"

Seeley's shoulders bobbed with a shrug. "No idea."

"Great." Erica sagged back into the barstool and wiped her greasy hands on her paint-splattered jeans. She tugged distractedly at the hem of her violet singlet before meeting Seeley's gaze. "How am I supposed to get out of this mess?"

"If it was me, I'd try being a little friendlier to those most upset. Maybe tell them your side of the story, so they don't think you're such a whore."

"Why thank you, Seeley," Erica rebuked. "Nothing makes my day more than being called a *whore* by my best friend."

"Calm yourself, crazy-pants." Seeley grabbed a bottle of tequila and poured out a shot. "Your drama is just the flavor of the month, but it will all blow over with the next commotion, you'll see."

"I'm going to hold you to that prediction, you know?"

As Seeley nodded, Erica watched her pour out a second shot of tequila.

"Just tell me one thing"—Seeley pushed a glass toward Erica—"was it worth all this trouble? Sex with Matt, I mean."

Erica smiled before she could calculate an appropriate reaction.

With a broad grin, Seeley held up her full shot glass, and then offered Erica a wink and a nod combination as though in salute. "That's what I wanted to hear," she said.

*

"Look out. The Hell-beast approaches." Nate's gaze dropped from the pathway which flowed alongside the alfresco seating of the Mountainview café. Standing quickly, he snatched his take-out coffee off their table. "I'm taping out. If you need me, I'll be over at Patrizio's browsing neckties." He pointed at the stylish menswear store across the quiet street.

"They're not even open yet." Matt's argument fell on deaf ears as Nate half-ran across the road, waving a hand in farewell, which quickly changed to a raised middle finger as he passed Seeley.

Even against the bright blaze of the early morning sun, Seeley raised her dark sunglasses, resting them atop her head to shoot Nate's back a blistering glare. They looked like polar opposites as they passed, Nate in his trendy navy trousers and white button-down, and Seeley in her torn, tight black jeans and checkered midriff top. It was no wonder they didn't get along.

"I'm guessing that display was for my benefit," she said when she reached Matt.

Seeing the agitation in her tired eyes and the sternness in the tight line of her lips, Matt's confidence level fell. He'd wanted this arranged meeting to go well, needed to make a good impression. Nate had known that, and yet, he'd still decided to harass the harpy. Not that Matt had any problem with Seeley, but her fiery reputation proceeded her, and today he really needed her help.

"Thanks for meeting with me, Seeley."

She yawned loudly, showing the world her tonsils, before taking a seat opposite him. "You're lucky I like you," she said gruffly. "I *never* get up before ten on a Friday."

While Seeley gestured to a waiter to place her coffee order, Matt hoped she knew how grateful he truly was. He'd contacted her late on Thursday, begging to catch up with her before the next life drawing class. Since getting another round of the cold shoulder from Erica after their romantic interlude on Monday night, he'd finally decided to listen to Nate's advice to get Seeley on his side. Maybe she could give him some insight into what he was doing wrong—or right? God knew he needed something—short of divine intervention.

When her blue eyes, like fierce flames, returned to his, they burned into him with challenge. Nerves had him skimming his hands over his khaki chinos before fiddling with the collar of his blue shirt.

"You said on the phone that you were desperate for my help."

Matt nodded.

"You want me to give you some tips on how to lock down my girl? How to get her to stop seeing you as a plaything?"

"Yes and no," he explained. "Erica likes me much more than she's letting on. I'm certain of it, but I need a way to convince her to take a chance on us."

"Sure thing, Romeo," Seeley sneered.

All the air felt as though it had been punched out of Matt's gut, and his posture deflated. As though noticing his reaction, Seeley sighed.

"Look, I know Erica likes you, and I know she *loves* the orgasms you're so skilled at giving her. That's enough to build a relationship on."

When the waiter arrived with Seeley's order in hand, she took a long, satisfying sip before continuing, "Erica's just afraid of repeating the cycle. She's convinced, because of past experiences, that all men will let her down eventually. I know better than to generalize, and that the only cycle she keeps repeating is that she chooses to fall in love with dipshits." Seeley leaned forward, sliding her elbows onto the white tabletop as she eyed him carefully. "You aren't a dipshit, Matt."

Matt's eyes narrowed on hers. "Thanks?"

Seeley nodded. "Deep down, I think Erica knows it, too. She knows you're good for her and that you're good together."

Lifting her coffee to her lips, Seeley took a sip and then shut those bright eyes of hers for a moment, as though relishing the taste. When she opened them again, they pierced Matt's like bolts of sharp blue electricity.

"You say you need to find a way to convince her to take a chance on the two of you, but she already has. She's still seeing you, still sleeping with you, still *wants* to see and sleep with you. It might not feel like a big deal to *you*, but it is to *her*. That's more of herself than she's given any other man for the past five years."

As Matt's heartbeat quickened, he leaned forward eagerly. He'd been craving to spend more time with Erica, aching to be closer to her, feeling as though what they'd had together just wasn't enough. And yet, for Erica it was a substantial change, a gigantic leap toward something more—even if she wasn't quite ready to acknowledge it.

Enlightened with this new information, Matt's lips twisted with a smile. "So, what? You're suggesting I keep doing what I'm already doing?"

"Matt, I'm telling you she's into you, but that she's still afraid. If you want to keep her, you'll have to be the one to open up, to tell her how you feel, to show her you care. To believe it's true, she has to get it back, so I'm suggesting you woo her, you seduce her, do all the things you believe will convince her of your affection—just do them at two hundred percent."

"That will work?"

Seeley relaxed back into her chair as she threaded her hands together and rested them behind her head. "It's a fine line. Too much and you'll scare her away for life. Too little and she'll stereotype you with all the others."

Matt shook his head and groaned. "Thanks, Seeley, but I can't figure out if your advice is meant to help me or hinder me."

"Hey," she exclaimed. "What's the point of true love if you don't fight for it?"

"You better have meant it when you said before that you like me," he told her. "I'd rather have you as an ally than an adversary in all of this."

Seeley chuckled and reached once again for her coffee. "Any friend of Nate's isn't usually a friend of mine." She took a quick sip. "But for you, I'll make an exception."

Matt laughed. "What is it with you two anyway?"

"He told all the boys in our kindergarten class that I ate boogers—and he's an all-round asshole."

Matt nodded slowly. "Right." The way he drew out the word had Seeley arching an eyebrow at him, so he quickly raised his hands in defense. "I'm not arguing, I just hadn't believed the feud was so ingrained."

"What's that supposed to mean?"

"He'd always told me you were born hostile, but now I'm starting to think the two of you came into the world sparring."

Seeley laughed whole-heartedly. "Damn straight, we did."

As Matt joined in her good humor, his thoughts drifted back to Seeley's suggestions.

Was it really that straightforward? Could just being there for Erica—being supportive, loyal, sharing every romantic and loving notion in order to prove just how much he cared, how dedicated he was to seeing their budding relationship flourish—be enough to get her to give him a chance?

It wasn't a difficult feat. That behavior was already ingrained in him. He'd never let any of his loved ones down and wasn't about to start a trend with the woman who was very easily his dream girl. If Seeley was correct in her assumptions, in Erica's expectations, then all Matt had to do was be himself, listen to his heart and do everything he could to show Erica just how truly perfect he believed they were for each other.

CHAPTER 17

Matt noticed Melina's concern as he entered the Hoffman Close Medical Practice at twenty past nine, but managed to make it all the way to the door of his office before she intervened.

"Is everything okay, Matthew?" Her voice was hushed as she hurried up beside him, her demure floral dress swishing around her. "It's not like you to be late."

"Everything's fine, Melina. My coffee date with a friend ran longer than expected, that's all."

Matt had taken his time with Seeley, drawing every sliver of information he could from her on how best to win Erica over. Although he'd deciphered the gist behind her riddle of advice, he hadn't felt content. He had needed specifics, and, even more than that, he'd needed reassurance.

What Matt had learned from Seeley had given him hope. Erica cared about him. Seeley was convinced her friend was, in the very least, harboring an avid crush on him, and that had boosted his confidence in a major way. Now all he had to do was put some plans in place to secure more than just her lust. He wanted all of her in his life, not only her body but her heart and soul, as well.

"Date?" Melina's tone rose an octave.

Matt slumped as he realized his mistake.

"Don't get too excited, Melina," Nate said as he appeared beside them. "He was only meeting up with Seeley."

Matt shot his friend a glare as Melina's hopeful smile faltered.

"Seeley? I thought you were seeing Erica? That's what Jocelyn told me."

Matt gritted his teeth tightly and shook his head. Thanks to Nate every woman in town would hear a similar version of his buddy's claim before the end of the day.

"Erica's such a nice girl," Melina continued, "but that Seeley can be wild. You know, Mrs. Marx told me she set her last boyfriend's clothes on fire. Just threw them in the gutter and lit up a match." She put her hands on her hips and *tsked*.

"It was a friendly catch-up, Melina." Matt smiled, touching her shoulder reassuringly. "Only a chat. No clothes were set on fire."

When she eyed him with skepticism, Matt glowered at Nate.

"And, where were you? What happened to tie shopping?"

Nate's sly smirk spoke volumes. "I got bored and then ran into Chloe."

Matt noticed Melina's lips purse, but before she could add her two cents' worth, he pointed back to the waiting room. The half-dozen nosy townspeople seated in that space immediately looked away, their gazes shifting back to their spouses, the magazines supplied, or even the ceiling. One older gentleman in a tartan beret actually began to whistle.

Melina sighed loudly as she turned away, but after a few steps, she faced them again and clicked her fingers. "Matthew, a delivery came for you before we opened. It was left on the front step. I've put it on your desk. I hope that's all right."

"Thanks, Melina."

Her expression warmed as she waggled her fingers at them, and then retreated.

When Matt met Nate's cheerful expression, he scowled at him. "Thanks a lot, buddy." He opened the door to his office. "I think the town's rumor mill has enough material without your contribution."

As Matt stepped into the cozy room and moved to close the door behind him, Nate slapped a hand against it, forcing it open so he could follow his friend inside.

"Hey, you're the one who decided to meet up with Seeley." Nate shut the office door and then slid his hands into the pockets of his navy trousers.

"Yeah. Well, you're the one who told me to," Matt snapped.

"You're the idiot who listened to me."

Matt's lips twitched with the urge to smile.

"Besides, I reckon it wasn't a total bust," Nate continued, whacking Matt amicably on the shoulder. "You came back chirpy, so she must've offered you something useful."

"I guess you could say she gave me hope."

Nate's attention drifted over his buddy's shoulder and his eyes widened. "Okay, and *who* gave you *that*?"

Frowning, Matt spun around to face his desk.

Just as Melina had said, she'd left the delivered item on top. Matt had been envisaging a parcel in a normal mailbag, maybe even a box. Since he hadn't been expecting anything in particular, he'd believed he'd find a package of medical supplies that had accidentally been addressed to him personally instead of the practice. Even something from his parents, who were happily retired and living back in Brisbane, wouldn't have been too much of a surprise. But this—he only wished Melina could have prepared him for it.

Similar to the red velvet cupcakes, this longer box—

twice the size of an ordinary shoebox—was wrapped in a pink and red love heart wrapping paper. On top of it sat a huge scarlet envelope also in the shape of a heart with his name scrawled in neat, ladylike handwriting on the front.

Matt was physically repulsed, his stomach lurching at the sight. He couldn't decide whether his reaction was due to the gaudiness of the exaggerated gift, the fact that his *secret admirer* was raising the stakes, or that he'd eventually have to let this person down by telling them he cared deeply for another. He was stressed enough about his desire to win Erica's heart. He didn't want to fret over emotionally injuring someone else, as well.

Matt glanced at Nate. "Still think it's the local real estate agent trying to butter me up?"

Nate shook his head and stepped closer to the garish monstrosity. "Depends on what's inside, really." His fingers went to the card before he fired a look back at Matt.

"Go ahead," Matt said as he took a wide berth around his desk and perched himself on the examination table. "I want nothing to do with it."

Nate laughed. "Even after those innocent cupcakes, you're still worried it might be something dangerous."

"Well, you're the one who's about to find out."

Ignoring Matt's warning, Nate slipped open the sleeve of the envelope and yanked out the huge heart-shaped card. From where he was seated, Matt could see by the intricate, decorative cover that the card was handmade. Nate's gaze lifted to his for an instant, almost seeking permission, and then he flipped it open.

"*To replace what was ruined on the night we had our first true moment together,*" Nate read aloud. "Any ideas?"

"You've taken the reins of this exploit, you work it out."

Nate rolled his eyes. Dropping the card to the desktop, he began tearing into the paper. It was only after he tore the majority from the box's lid, revealing a company name and logo below, that recognition hit Matt.

"Wait." He jumped off the table and moved beside Nate. "I know that brand."

Nate read the label on the box. "Hardcastle?"

"It's a bespoke tailor in Sydney. I bought a few items from them a few years back when on holiday."

Matt carefully lifted the white lid of the stylish box. After shifting a mass of silver tissue paper, he noted the smooth, gray fabric of a familiar piece of clothing and drew the item free. It was the same shirt he'd worn to the life drawing class last Friday, the same shirt he'd been wearing when he'd returned to Unique Art Boutique later that night, and the *same shirt* he'd ruined when he'd torn it off himself to get naked with Erica for the very first time.

Nate touched a smooth gray sleeve. "It's a dress shirt."

Desperate to elucidate the item's importance, Matt opened his mouth to answer but spluttered as he tried to swallow and breathe in all at once. Matt dropped the garment into the box and stepped backward, his whole-body convulsing as he coughed.

"You all right, buddy?" Nate slapped Matt on the back in an effort to clear his airways.

Matt nodded and finally stopped coughing. Straightening, he breathed deeply.

"Thank God." Nate chuckled. "For a split-second there, I was thinking anthrax."

"I think it might be worse." Matt's voice was hoarse.

"It's just a shirt, buddy. How could it be worse?"

Matt's heart raced, his skin becoming cool and clammy. He took another calming breath before glancing down at the elaborately decorated crimson and pink card on the desk. "I own the exact same shirt. It got damaged last Friday night, the first night Erica and I got together."

A smile pulled at his friend's lips, but Matt shook his head.

"No, Erica didn't send this. I think someone else was there that night, watching us."

CHAPTER 18

"Stop fiddling, Erica. It looks fine." Seeley berated her from across the small table they'd set up in the middle of Unique Art Boutique's classroom. "No one's going to care if a pretty flower is facing this way or that, all eyes will be on the boys—and you, if you're not careful."

Erica stopped fussing with the botanical arrangement she'd organized for the night's life drawing class and straightened. Squaring her shoulders, she smoothed the material of her turquoise halter top. "Do I have to remind you again that I haven't done anything wrong?"

"Of course not." Seeley grinned. "You slept with one of the most eligible bachelors in town, essentially taking him off the market, even though you're not keen to pursue a proper relationship with him. What's wrong with that?"

Scowling, Erica moved her hands to her denim-clad hips. "I can't tell whether you're criticizing my behavior or if you're pleased by it?"

"I'd be a whole lot more *pleased* if you'd just decide to date the poor guy."

"Don't you think it would be best for everyone, including him, if I just left him alone?"

Seeley shook her head slowly. "I don't think that's what

131

he wants, do you?"

Erica waved a hand dismissively and made her way through the maze of desks to the workbench where she'd left her mobile phone. It was vibrating with yet another silent incoming call from an unknown number. Holding the button on the side, she switched it off.

"Let me guess, another sexy text message from Dr. Loverboy?"

"No." Erica poked out her tongue.

Seeley's lips curled back as though she were looking at something grotesque. "That unknown number then?"

Erica nodded, her stomach churning unsettlingly. The calls had become incessant and had even spread to the shop's phone. She'd had to unplug it to escape the unrelenting ringing. Seeley had agreed with her that it was no longer likely to be a client desperate to make contact, but could be one of the many women in town Erica had offended when she'd made a move on Matt.

"I still reckon you should call the police," Seeley suggested as she arranged acid-free paper and an assortment of pencils at each desk and easel. "That would scare the crap out of whichever wannabe-wife is responsible."

"Don't you think I've already upset these women enough? I'm just hoping this will all blow over if I can manage to show them I'm not a threat."

Seeley's booming laughter shook the entire shop. "You?" She brushed joyous tears from her eyes and then wiped her damp fingers on her ebony jeans. "Not a threat?" She struggled to catch her breath. "Don't be ridiculous. You're the only contender."

When Erica glowered at her, Seeley quietened down but continued.

"Those other women might think they have a chance, but I saw the way Matt looked at you last week—and that was before you slept with him. In his eyes, this is a one-horse race, and he's just waiting for you to get to the finish line and claim your prize."

"I don't know where you get this stuff, Seels, but you're not helping."

Seeley smiled sweetly and, leaving the pencils and paper on a desk, headed over to Erica. "Of course, I am." She reached her, patting Erica's bare shoulder reassuringly. "The sooner you admit to what you can and can't change, the sooner you'll be taking Matt out on a proper date and placating the villagers with friendliness."

Erica opened her mouth, prepared to retort, but Seeley was saved by the *tinkling* of the little bell on the front door. Seeing Diana and Lauren wander in, Erica glanced back to her mischievous friend.

"Why don't you finish setting up, while I go *placate the villagers?*"

Seeley snorted, appearing more irritated by the interruption than by Erica's remark but did as instructed.

"Ladies." Erica hurried around the static shelving, greeting the two young women loitering in the store with her brightest grin. "How are you doing this evening?"

It took a moment for Lauren to meet Erica's gaze. "Sorry we're early, Erica. We—"

"We wanted to get good seats," Diana interjected. "I hope that's okay."

"Sure. That's absolutely fine. Seeley's almost finished arranging everything, if you'd like to go in now."

Diana met Lauren's eyes before stepping closer to Erica. "Is *she* in a good mood tonight?" Diana bobbed her head in Seeley's direction.

"Seeley?"

Diana nodded.

Erica grimaced. "She's ... Seeley, but I'll make sure she's on her best behavior."

Diana bit her lip and nodded once more before leading Lauren into the classroom.

As she followed them in, Erica noted their casual but pretty attire. Lauren's yellow sundress and Diana's denim jeans and fuchsia blouse were innocent in comparison to many of the suggestive, flesh-baring outfits she'd noticed on some of her students last week. Seeley had described Diana as *dangerously* competitive, and yet, Erica just couldn't see that in the other woman. They had both always been friendly to her, although a little reserved, and that had Erica considering Seeley's previous advice.

Maybe she really should make-nice with the women in town, at least some of them anyway, in the hopes of making amends? And maybe if the town grapevine got a hold of her side of the story, the relentless calls would finally cease? That idea brought a smile to her lips.

"Ladies," Erica announced, drawing their attention as they took seats on the far side of the room. "Seeley and I were just talking about having a movie night."

"We were?"

"Yes." Erica grinned at her best friend. "We were, and we thought it might be nice to invite some of the younger women in town over to my place for a bit of a girls' night. What do you think? Are you interested?"

"A girls' night?" Diana shot a wary glance at Lauren, but her friend just beamed.

"Of course, Erica. It would be wonderful to spend more time with you."

At her companion's eager agreement, Diana forced a nod, a small smile plastered to her face, before her gaze flashed nervously at Seeley again.

Glowering her displeasure at Erica, Seeley just growled. "Oh, this is going to be great fun."

Erica risked another glance in Matt's direction only to discover he was still staring at her as she paced slowly around the circle of desks and easels. The last two hours had been the same. While several of her students tittered, some of the women quietly flirting with Nate, attempting to do the same with Matt, and the rest worked diligently on their artwork, Matt had kept his gaze securely on hers and her constant migration around the room.

She'd noticed him sketching, had seen glimpses of his creation over his shoulder, and yet it baffled her how he'd penciled anything when his eyes always seemed fixed to hers. Never once had she seen him looking at the elegant vase of colorful tulips and peonies. It had made her wonder what he'd even drawn on his sheet of paper.

"Okay, everyone." Erica's calm voice disturbed the muffled scratch of pencil on paper and the gentle hum of light indistinct chatter. "Pencils down. Well done. I saw a lot of concentration and passion around the room tonight." Her words were met with several stifled giggles. "You should all be very proud of what you've achieved. I hope you're all keen to bring that same enthusiasm next week."

There were sounds of affirmation, some nods, and a few more chuckles as people began to stand or shift in their seats in preparation to leave. Pencils rattled against the timber of the desks with some falling and tapping on the floor as easels, chairs, and tables scraped and rasped over the wooden floorboards.

On the other side of the room, Seeley jumped up from where she'd been lounging in a tattered armchair. When she hadn't been watching the flock like a suspicious ewe trying to spot the wolf dressed as a sheep, she'd been wasting the time away by flicking through an ancient women's fitness magazine. As she neared Erica, she snatched her smartphone from the back pocket of her torn, ebony jeans. The screen came alive, illuminating her features in its glow and making her smile.

"Good news?" Erica asked her when Seeley reached her side.

"Nothing special."

"Message from Tom?"

Seeley shrugged. "Maybe."

"I thought you said he wasn't your type?"

"He's not," Seeley snapped.

Maybe not, but Erica was starting to suspect that fact didn't matter anymore. Maybe Seeley was becoming cured of her predilection for bad boys?

"What did he want then?"

A smile tugged at Seeley's lips. "To meet me for a drink at the Tavern."

Erica's heart did an excited little flip-flop in her chest for her best friend. "And you're still here because?"

"Because having me around is like a deterrent for any crazies—and I promised to help you clean up."

Erica gestured to the majority of students who were already filing out of the classroom, their artwork in hand as they headed for the front door. Only Nate, his usual small entourage, as well as Diana, Lauren, and Matt, who'd been caught in Tonya's clutches again, remained.

"I think I'm pretty safe with these guys," Erica told her. "Except maybe Matt, and you know that's for another reason entirely."

Before Seeley had the opportunity to respond, Erica raised both hands, balancing them in the air as though weighing options.

"As for staying to help me clean up"—Erica raised one hand purposely higher than the other—"surely having the opportunity to hang out with a nice, attractive man trumps that."

"It's not a date, you know?" Seeley informed her.

"Oh, I know."

Seeley watched her for a moment and then nodded. "Fine." She waved a hand in the air, indicating the mess of tables, easels, paper, and utensils still littering the room. "Are you going to leave all of this for tomorrow?"

"There's no need." Lauren piped up beside them. "Diana and I can give you a hand cleaning up, Erica. It's no trouble."

Their keen smiles had Erica pondering. Was it possible that the promise of a movie night together had already endeared her to them?

"See. I'll be fine, Seels." As Erica smirked in Seeley's direction, her friend shot the other two women a wary look.

"I hope Erica's told you there's no need to stay, ladies." Matt's deep voice interrupted them all, making Erica jump. He only grinned as he stepped beside her and rested a possessive hand low on her back. "Thank you for offering to help, but Erica and I, we have it handled."

"We?" Erica spluttered.

She glanced from the solemn expressions of her new friends, past the amusement in Seeley's cheerful eyes, and over to the self-assuredness on Matt's face. She quickly shifted out of his embrace, freeing herself from the touch that burned and tingled through the material of her clothes and into her skin.

Matt's face flinched slightly before he turned his attention back to Diana and Lauren. "Have a wonderful night, ladies. We hope to see you next week."

We? There was that word again. *We!* There was no *we*. It was only her and him, separately. This was *her* shop, *her* class, not *theirs*.

Her blood boiled, her cheeks blushing with building rage as she watched Lauren and Diana turn and head toward the exit.

Had Matt ruined her chance to become friends with them? And for that matter, her chance to repair her reputation and stop those incessant calls?

Clearly, he was intent on destroying her happy, little life as the few men before him had been. But instead of cheating on her, being suffocatingly controlling or having unattainable standards, he was refusing to take her "no" for the answer it was. *No*, they couldn't have a relationship. *No*, they shouldn't have a relationship. And *no*, she wasn't quite sure if she wanted one.

But, did she?

Her anger cooled slightly. Would things have been

easier if she'd said *yes* and they'd entered into a proper loving relationship? Would she still have received the harassing phone calls? Would there have been less animosity toward her from the women in town? Would she have been happier? Would *they* have been happier?

She shook her head and glared over at Matt, hating that the tenderness in his eyes made her heart flutter. "Thanks a lot," she growled. "Do you want every woman in town to hate me?"

"I don't care about the other women in town. I only care about you."

With a huff, she threw up her hands and then looked at Seeley.

"Don't look at me," Seeley all but laughed at her. "You gave me permission to go catch up with Tom remember?" She placed a hand on Erica's bare shoulder. "I'm sure you'll both have plenty of time to talk this issue through while you clean."

Erica slapped the hand away. "Some friend you are," she sniffed before nodding toward the front door. "Off with you then."

With a wave good-bye, Seeley took her opportunity to exit. It was only when Erica turned back to Matt, ready to give him a piece of her mind, that she realized they weren't yet alone. Nate and his awesome foursome—Chloe, Anabelle, Nicolette, and Tonya—were all observing the display with interest. It was just a shame Erica wasn't keen on PDA—public displays of aggression—as it meant Matt had escaped her wrath this round and would just have to wait until later to cop the argument he deserved.

CHAPTER 19

Matt was hot on Erica's heels like a puppy trailing its master. She'd hoped to lose him as she locked up the shop, hoped he'd head up Main Street with Nate and the all-girl cult which had made the taller, ranger man their leader, but had had no luck.

As she hit the unlock button on her car keys, the front and rear lights of her cute, red hatchback winked at her in the dim-lit backstreet.

"You know, my car was closer," he told her, his voice all deep, velvety tones.

"As if I'm going to fall for that again," Erica spat over her shoulder.

She picked up her pace as she neared the safety of the vehicle, but heard the heavy slap of his shoes on the pavement behind her. Matt jogged in front of her to the driver's side door and then leaned his broad, muscular body against the metal and plastic frame, blocking her path.

"Weren't we supposed to have a chat?" He asked when she reached him.

Erica grabbed for the door handle, but he shifted quickly until it was hidden beneath the firmness of his backside. She scowled up into his handsome face, into those gold-speckled eyes, and did her best to remain unintimidated, even though her excited heartbeat proved otherwise.

"We were, until your friend and his harem decided to stay and help tidy, as well."

"That wasn't my fault." He raised his hands, palms out, in defense. "I told Nate to leave us in peace."

"Yeah, then he said he wouldn't leave until he was sure I was going to be nice to you."

Matt stifled a chuckle. "I'm almost certain he stayed for his own selfish interests." He rested his elbows on the roof of her car. "You see, the twins are becoming scarily competitive with Nicolette, and Tonya told me tonight that she's got a *thing* for him. I think Nate only stayed because he didn't want to end up alone with all of them together. I'm guessing that's why they're heading to the Tavern, so he won't be by himself if a catfight breaks out."

Erica wasn't quick enough to conceal her smirk. "I feel like I'm letting down womankind by not disputing that, by letting the desperate single woman stereotype thrive, but— they all really like him, don't they?"

Matt nodded. "I think they do, but Nate's stuck on one a little more than the others. That's why it's becoming more difficult for him. He just hasn't told me which one."

"Maybe he doesn't want to jinx it."

Matt's attractive eyes examined her very closely. "Is that what you're doing?"

Erica's breath caught in her throat. She glanced down at the back of her bare wrist as though checking the dial on a watch. "Look at the time," she exclaimed. "It's too late for a deep and meaningful. Sorry." She stepped closer and tried to reach around him for the door handle.

As her hand wedged between the cold metal of the door and the firmness of his butt cheek, she found herself staring into his ardent gaze, her lips barely a breath from his.

"I *know* it's not too late for this," he told her as he touched his warm hands to her jaw, her neck, pulling her to him, his mouth meeting hers in a sensual bite.

Erica got lost in the sensation, in the hungry but seductive dance of his tongue as it caressed her, in the taste of him, the intoxicating smell of his skin. Her whole body throbbed, her breasts swelling, aching to be touched, while the twinge deep in her belly craved to have those kisses placed somewhere much lower.

When he ended the kiss, he slipped his hands down around her waist to lock her body against his. Erica felt completely dazed, her head swooning from the passionate attack. Matt placed another gentle peck to her lips and tried to catch her gaze as her eyes fluttered open.

"What were you saying?"

Once her wits had returned, she glared at him. "I hate you."

"I feel the same way." He kissed the tip of her nose.

Erica wrinkled it at the ticklish touch. "Are you ever going to let me go home, or are you planning on seducing me in the street?"

Matt's eyes sparkled as he dipped his hands lower and grasped her backside, forcing her hips to his so she could feel the bulge between them. "I'm up for the challenge, if you are?"

"Sorry, but I draw the line at public nudity."

"Oh, well. Looks like we'll have to head to your place instead."

Erica tried to decide whether or not he was joking.

"We're not having another sleepover," she warned him. "I can drop you off at your place on the way. Or you could do the chivalrous thing and head back to your own car."

He gave her a charming, pearly-white grin, and she gnawed on her lower lip.

He wasn't about to do either, was he?

*

Matt was beginning to wonder just how long their standoff was going to last. After he'd persuaded Erica to take him with her, she'd refused to start driving until he offered up his address. At the time he'd thought of relinquishing the information as a defeat, but when they'd arrived shortly after, he'd considered it meant to be. No matter what obstacles she put in the way, he was going to make every effort to spend more time with her tonight.

Matt knew Erica liked him, if the sizzling chemistry and the mind-blowing sex weren't enough to convince him, then remembering his conversation with Seeley did the trick. Even though Erica wasn't willing to admit it yet, to him, to herself, her best friend knew the truth. She could see it in her eyes, in her telling smiles, in the tone of her voice when she spoke of him. Erica was stuck on him, and Heaven Almighty, he was stuck on her.

"Are you intending to get out some time before dawn?" Erica's voice oozed sarcasm as she sat in the driver's seat, her hands gripping the steering wheel while she stared straight ahead at Matt's faintly-lit apartment block.

"It depends," he said, trying to catch her eye, "are you getting out with me?"

"Let me think?" Her gaze flew to his as she tapped her index finger against her mouth, her loose bun of dark chocolate hair jiggling with the abrupt movement. Then she pointed at him. "*This* is where *you* live." She turned her index finger on herself. "*I* don't live here. Does that answer your question?"

When his lips tugged into a smirk, he licked them to hide it. "Not really. Maybe you should try it again?"

Rage radiated from her gorgeous brown eyes.

"Come on, I'll help you," he prodded her gently. "Erica, would you like to come up to my place for coffee and a chat?"

"Don't you ever give up?"

Matt's satisfied smile reached his eyes. "Forgive me if I'm wrong, but that didn't sound like a *no*."

She looked like she could've slapped him, but she kept her white-knuckled fists clenched around the steering wheel. "There's a difference between not wanting to do something and knowing you shouldn't."

"And why shouldn't you be able to have an innocent coffee with me?"

Her eyes darkened. "You and I both know it wouldn't be innocent."

"And that's a problem because?"

"Like I've told you before," she said, releasing her tight hold on the steering wheel so she could turn in her seat to face him, "I'm not looking for a relationship."

"Well, aren't you lucky that one found you instead?"

Erica's glare in response was icy.

Matt reached out and took her hand in his, surprised for just a moment that she let him without making a fuss. "I know you're worried your life will change if you let me in, Erica, but I don't want to take over. I just want to be *with* you, get to know you, care for you, support you and your dreams. For me, that's what a relationship is about. Sharing your life with your partner."

She eyed her hand in his, watching as he stroked the soft skin of her palm.

"Can't you at least give me a chance?" Matt hated hearing the lilt of fear in his voice.

Whether she agreed to it or not, he'd fight for her. There was enough between them to prove to him that they had something special, and if Erica needed more time, needed further convincing, then he would do his best to give it to her. He thought when he'd first seen her that she was a good match for him, and now he was certain of it.

It seemed to take an eternity for her to lift her gaze to his, but when she did, he saw something positive there—a glimmer of hope.

"I have to ask you a serious question." It seemed a

strain for her just to say those few words.

"More serious than mine?" When she frowned at him, he nodded at her. "Sure."

"Do you have feelings for any of the other women in town?"

The look of astonishment that had Matt's brows lifting and his mouth twisting must have been an impressive sight, because Erica was quick to continue before he could respond.

"It might sound silly to you, but I need to know." She took a steadying breath. "I feel as though in starting something with you, I've let everyone else down. A lot of those women at the class tonight care about you, have even imagined a future with you because of this whole life drawing dating night farce."

Even though he knew she had a point and had witnessed some of the overeager behavior herself, he shook his head at her reassuringly.

"I need to know that you're sure there's no connection for you there," Erica continued, "that I'm not ruining your opportunity to have something easier, something more definite with one of the other incredible ladies in town."

Again, Matt shook his head. How could she even think he could have feelings for anyone else? He'd met the majority of women in Montville through Nate's dating escapades and never once had he felt a soulful attraction, that spark of desire he'd been hit with upon meeting her. It had been Erica that his heart beat boldly for, for whom his heart came alive for.

"You have to tell me the truth, Matt," she told him on a sigh, "because I can't promise you anything. We're friends. I like you, and I like sleeping with you." Her gaze dropped briefly from his. "I *really* like sleeping with you, but I'm not ready to share my life with you."

When her eyes connected with his again, Matt realized she was finally ready to hear him out.

"Erica," he crooned her name affectionately. "I am not

and have never been interested in any of the other women in this town." He held up his free hand to pause any reservations. "*Even* if they have imagined a future together with me. If I'm interested in any kind of relationship, it's with you, and whatever you can offer me now is better than not having you in my life at all."

She frowned and toyed with his fingers, glancing down at her hand still in his as she did so. "I feel like I'm cheating you out of true happiness."

He laughed at that. "Being with you brings me true happiness, Erica. As long as I know you're willing to let me in little by little, that you're content to give me a chance, then I will give you as much time as you need to realize I'm the *one* for you."

Her wide, dark eyes shot back to his. "I don't like it when you say things like that."

"Why? It's true."

She swallowed deeply. "It sounds like I don't have a choice in the matter."

"Sometimes destiny makes the choice for you," he whispered.

Matt knew better than to let her dwell on that thought. He pulled her close and pressed his lips to the softness of hers.

CHAPTER 20

Matt would have noticed it sooner had he not been so engrossed in the sweetness of Erica's kisses or by his desire to get her inside his apartment before she changed her mind. It was only after he shut the door behind them and propped Erica on the kitchen countertop that he recognized something was amiss.

His hot blood, ablaze with lust, ran suddenly cold at the sight of yet another gift from his secret admirer. He broke free of Erica's ardent embrace to peer down at the small, neatly wrapped box about the size of his palm.

"What?" Erica was staring at him. "What's wrong? Are you okay?"

Eyes still wide in horror, Matt looked from her to the pink and red love heart paper covering the box. Erica's gaze followed his, and she jumped down from the benchtop when she saw what she was sitting next to. Grabbing her hand, Matt pulled her over to him protectively.

"What is it, Matt?"

"Another surprise, I guess." He frowned, but still didn't go near the box.

Matt wanted to call Nate, to make him come over and

open it since he was always so keen. Or call the police and ask for the bomb squad, but that option seemed too excessive, and in all honesty, he didn't want to overreact when the whole situation could be completely innocent. Sure, the box was inside his apartment, inside his private dwelling, which meant someone would've had to trespass on his privacy to leave it there. But Montville was a small country town and he was new here. For all he knew, this kind of behavior could be commonplace. After all, it wasn't as though he was the only one with a key. His landlord had the master, and Matt had given Nate and Melina a copy in case of emergencies. It seemed more likely for one of them to have noticed this on his doorstep and taken it inside.

"Another surprise?" Erica inched forward. "You mean this isn't the first one?"

Matt shook his head. "This is the third. So far, they've all been relatively harmless. Some cupcakes, a dress shirt, and now whatever this is."

"A dress shirt?"

Glancing back at her, Matt watched her closely, taking in the disbelief in her intense brown eyes. He mused back to the present he'd received earlier that day and the note which had accompanied it.

To replace what was ruined on the night we had our first true moment together, it had read.

At the time it had unnerved him so much he'd actually considered that someone else may have been watching during his first passionate encounter with Erica. It wasn't until Nate had enlightened him, mentioning that there were likely several women in attendance that night who believed they'd had a moment with him and reminded him of the unnatural velocity of the town's gossip grapevine, that Matt began to think more clearly. One of his "fans" could have seen him heading back to his car the morning after, shirt torn, buttons missing. It was possible they'd later heard of the night's events and had bought him the shirt in an effort to bribe their way into his heart. Or perhaps there was a more obvious answer?

Matt looked into Erica's dark eyes. Although he'd seriously doubted she was behind the girlishly romantic and somewhat juvenile gifts, he had never actually clarified it. "Can you bake?" He asked her.

"If my life depended on it, yes. Why are you asking?"

He sighed. "I'd feel a lot more at ease if I knew it was you doing all of this." He gestured to where the scarlet and pink box remained on the countertop.

She grimaced. "Sorry, Matt, but it's not me. I've never been one to play secret admirer. If I'm asking to spend time with you, then you know where my heart is."

"Good to know. So, when you're the one calling me, following me around town, then I know it's real love?"

"Were you just born a smartass, or did Nate turn you into one?"

Matt laughed, but with the mystery still evident, his humor didn't last long. Looking back over at the box, he frowned. "If you aren't responsible, then who is?"

"I don't know?" Erica dropped his hand as she stepped closer to the gaudy offering. "A pastry chef with a keen sense of style who enjoys gift wrapping in their downtime?"

Again, Matt laughed. "Do you have a pastry chef in town who has a keen sense of style and gift wraps as their favorite pastime?"

She turned back to roll her eyes at him. "Don't be silly."

Matt threw up his hands. "Then, I'm all out of ideas."

Erica smirked at him. "Maybe you could try opening it to see if there's a return to sender address?"

"Highly doubtful." He stepped beside her. "I'm guessing anonymity is rule number one in the secret admirer handbook."

She pushed playfully at his shoulder. "Shut up and open it, or I will."

Grasping the gift between his fingers, Matt turned it around before noting there appeared to be two pieces. Lifting up the lid, adorned in the same brightly-colored paper as the bottom, he popped it free from the other half very slowly. Though a part of him was eager to know what the present was, he still had a niggling feeling that something might explode if he wasn't careful.

"No way." Erica peered inside. "Someone bought you a *keychain*?"

Matt tossed the wrapped lid on the countertop and snatched out the small jeweled plaque by its silver chain.

A key chain? Why did that sound so familiar to him?

Red gems lined the matchbox-sized tile of silver, while one heart-shaped jewel sat neatly in the center surrounded by the curly cursive of the inscription.

True love endures all, it read.

"Someone's pretty confident they're going to win you over," Erica told him.

Something tweaked into place in Matt's mind. Keychain? *Keys*? His misplaced keys. He'd told Nate about that incident.

"Could it really be that simple?" He'd said the words aloud, considering the possibility as he dropped the shiny present back into the box.

"Could *what* be that simple?" Erica rested a hand on his shoulder, drawing his gaze to hers.

"Nate was here when I received the cupcakes," he explained. "In fact, he saw them first. He also made it to the office before me this morning and was there with me when I opened the second gift and found the shirt."

"And that's strange because?" She tilted her head causing a dark strand of hair to fall across her cheek.

Before she could brush it back, Matt found it first and did it for her. Her skin was like silk as he skimmed his fingertips across her face and caressed the curve of her ear. He watched Erica's eyes close as she shivered at his fleeting touch. His heartbeat quickened and an eager need quivered low in his belly.

"It's strange because," he said, drawing her gaze to his once more, "Nate was also aware that I'd misplaced my house keys recently. Don't you think the keychain seems a little bit coincidental?"

Erica looked from him to the small box in his hand and then back again. "You think Nate's playing a practical joke on you?"

Matt nodded. Nate had been known for his antics in college, and though none had been quite this well organized, Matt wouldn't think him incapable. After all, the appearance of the mystery gifts had begun shortly after Matt had turned down another opportunity to go speed-dating due to the overeager participants. Perhaps this was just another way for his buddy to torment him about all the unwanted interest he'd received.

Frowning, Erica reached inside the little gift box and removed the keychain. "Do you really think he'd go to these lengths? It's pretty elaborate. Surely he's got better things to do with his time."

Leaving the bottom half of the package on the countertop beside him, Matt moved around Erica until he was standing behind her, peering over her shoulder at the sparkling silver plaque. Relief had his whole body relaxing, lifting his confidence and reigniting his desire.

"I can't say I'm certain." His breath disturbed the down-like hair at the base of Erica's skull, causing goosebumps to sprout over her kissable skin. "I'd have to confront him to be sure, but it seems very likely."

"*Very* likely?" She turned her head in an effort to glance back at him, but he took advantage of her closeness and pressed a light kiss to her pink lips.

He snuck his hands around her waist, locking together beneath her navel as he hugged her against him, before turning her slightly in his arms to get a better view of her beautiful face.

"You're very confident about this."

"The revelation of my secret admirer?" Again, he caught her mouth with his, kissing her sweetly before sucking her full lower lip between his teeth for an instant. Then he nodded to her, gesturing to the position they were in. "Or this?"

She clasped at his arms still around her waist while she caught her breath. "I could say *both*, but I meant the whole surprise gifts fiasco. You were pretty concerned about it a moment ago, and now, it's as if you've got the situation under control."

He shrugged but didn't let her go. "I think I do."

She smelled so divine, her hair, the sweet scent of her skin.

"Whether it is Nate or some hopeful soul, I really don't care. I'd rather not focus any more of my attention on them when I've got the woman of my dreams alone with me in my apartment and in my arms for the entire night."

At his words, something flickered in her dark eyes. Was it amusement? Or excitement? Maybe even affection?

As Erica's mouth rose to meet his, Matt knew it didn't matter either way. For tonight, he was content to have her, to hold her, and to fall further in love with her.

CHAPTER 21

"So, are you the good twin or the evil one?" Seeley didn't look up as she added more barbeque sauce to her steak burger.

Erica glanced up from the screen of her smartphone. She ceased wildly tapping her thumbs in a rhythmic dance. "What are you talking about, Seels?"

They sat opposite each other at an umbrella-covered wooden table on the green, fake-grass lawn of the Montville Tavern's outdoor setting. The Tuesday lunch crowd was minimal and mainly tourists, but it was known to build as the afternoon progressed and working shifts ended. Erica had needed their usual catch-up during the peace and quiet before Seeley's shift, but she had yet to broach what she wanted to.

"Well, with all that texting, you're definitely not my bestie, Erica," Seeley shot back as she smushed the brown sauce-coated bun back on top of the rest of her burger. "Maybe you're her evil twin?"

Feeling her cheeks grow warm, Erica turned her phone screen-down on the tabletop, pushing it away before dragging her own plated burger in front of her. "I was only replying."

Seeley raised the enormous, soggy atrocity of a steak burger up to her lips but paused before taking a bite. "You've *replied* like five times already." When she bit into the squelchy mess, honey brown sauce dribbled down her chin as she chewed. "Bet I know to who, too."

Grimacing, Erica ignored the mouthful of half-chewed food she'd just witnessed and handed her friend a pile of napkins. "So, what? We're friends. I reply to friends." She glared pointedly at Seeley. "I always reply to *you*."

Seeley rolled her eyes and swallowed loudly. "Sure, you're *friends*." She waved a couple of fingers free of her burger, gesturing over Erica's shoulder. "Just like Tonya and Nate over there want to be better *friends*."

Erica snatched a french fry from her plate and nibbled at it before turning to look in the direction. The tasty piece of fried potato nearly dropped from her fingertips at the sight.

Nate was canoodling with Tonya at a table partially shielded by a flowering hedge on the far side of the courtyard. She remembered Matt telling her Tonya was interested in Nate but hadn't really given it a second thought. Tonya was usually attracted to most flesh and blood males, so Matt's news hadn't been much of a revelation. Yet, the way Tonya was staring at Nate, the way she was stroking his hair, touching his face, it appeared less like her usual seduction tactics and more like genuine affection.

When Erica turned back to Seeley, she noticed her friend was now dabbing a scrunched napkin at a fresh brown stain on her crimson T-shirt.

"That's what you get for drowning a great meal in sauce."

Seeley's frosty scowl in response only made Erica laugh.

"Okay, let's change the subject." Erica picked at her fries and poked at her half-eaten burger. "I need to ask you a favor."

Seeley's gaze narrowed on her friend as she wiped her grubby fingers on the already dirty napkin. "I'm thinking *no* should be my answer to the next question."

"That's not very nice," Erica scolded. "You should at least hear me out."

Tossing her filthy napkin on the table beside her plate, Seeley sighed. "Fine."

Erica batted her eyelashes. "You know how we've organized a movie night with the girls this Saturday—"

"You've," Seeley interrupted curtly. "As in *you have*."

"And who was it who told me I should try being friendlier to the women in town to mend fences?"

When Seeley huffed in response, Erica lifted a piece of fried potato to her lips and bit off the end triumphantly.

"Okay, get on with it," Seeley growled.

"I know we had a deal. You promised to invite Tonya and a couple of her friends so I don't have to and then you don't have to play hostess with me."

"No," Seeley corrected, raising her index finger in protest. "The deal was that I didn't have to come."

"Well," Erica drew out the word in a lengthy bell-like sound.

"I knew it." Seeley threw up her hands. "You still want me to come."

"Pretty please?"

"I'm not playing hostess."

"Of course. That's fine. Just come."

After another drawn-out sigh, obviously more for Erica's benefit than her own, a touch of a smile pricked Seeley's lips. "You don't want to face them alone, do you?"

"Maybe."

"Worried they might bore you to death?"

Even though she coughed out a laugh, Erica's stomach churned uncomfortably as an icy chill raced up her spine. "Something like that," she said as she glanced down to where her smartphone was vibrating around on the tabletop.

"Still getting those calls?" There was concern in Seeley's voice as she snatched up Erica's phone, tapped the screen with her thumb, and lifted it to her ear.

"No, Seeley. Wait!"

"Hi, you've reached Madame Madeline's Boudoir Brothel where bits of all shapes and sizes come together in your most moist of fantasies. How may I direct your call?" Her pleased expression became a frown as she removed the mobile phone from her ear to return it. "They hung up."

"They always do," Erica agreed. "What made you think your spiel was going to change that?"

Seeley shrugged. "I have a way with women."

"Sure, you do."

"Well, you must think so or else you wouldn't have begged me to come protect you on Saturday."

"Har-har," Erica said, tilting her head from side to side with each sound.

At Seeley's satisfied grin, Erica stared down at the device in her hand. The screen had locked and turned dark, but she could still see the gray balloon in the center listing her missed calls. All of them were from an unknown number.

"Don't stress." Seeley reached across the table and took Erica's hand in hers. "It'll be sorted after Saturday. You'll see. Whoever it is will get their knickers untwisted and cut out this crap."

"I hope so."

"Now"—Seeley released Erica's hand to pick up the sloppy burger—"I've got meat to eat and a man to discuss. Tell me more about what's been happening with you and your man-friend with *big* benefits."

Though Erica rolled her eyes, it was times like these that she was wholeheartedly grateful for her friend's unabashed confidence. She just prayed to Heaven that Seeley was right.

Erica's home mailbox was unusually full. While she didn't always check it every day, sometimes out of laziness, often because there was rarely much, Tuesdays were different because of the junk mail delivery of store catalogs. However, there was more than just the usual recycling bin fodder in this afternoon's collection. After flicking through the assortment, she shoved the pile into her work bag before climbing back into her car. As she drove down the lush tree-lined, gravel driveway, which stretched a winding trail to her quaint country-style house, she noticed the stress and tension in her limbs had begun to decrease.

After finishing lunch with Seeley, Erica had met Jocelyn back at Unique Art Boutique for a private tutorial, something she'd been dreading most of the day. While Jocelyn had loved putting her two cents' worth in about Erica's "budding romantic relationship" between brushstrokes, Erica had worked hard to keep the true status of her and Matt's friends-with-benefits arrangement to herself. Unfortunately for her, all that repression had caused her muscles to become vice-like, and now all she longed to do was relax.

When Erica's wonderful, little brown and red brick cottage appeared in the windshield, her chest swelled, a contented sigh escaping her lips as she felt all those tight tendons ease their constriction. Her own home was something she'd always wanted, the stability, the security and independence, but something she hadn't been able to achieve until she'd taken herself out of the dating scene. Although it was nice to have Jocelyn—someone besides Seeley—in support of her and Matt's relationship, it had also made Erica fearful.

She knew Matt was right; they had something special together, but that didn't mean she was ready to put her whole happy life or her finally-mended heart in jeopardy. She wanted to believe he was different, that he meant what he said and that his feelings were true. Really, she did. As he'd told her, he deserved a chance, and that's exactly what she was trying to give him—only in friendship first.

After jumping out of the car to open the shed-like garage, adjacent to the house, Erica parked her vehicle inside before securing the roller door shut. Slinging the strap of her work bag over her shoulder, she admired the comfortable, mauvy gloom that the setting sun had created in the shadows of the tall trees which surrounded her home. Tonight, she was going to take it easy, maybe have a bath, drink some wine, and go to bed early.

As she climbed the couple of steps up to the porch, she grabbed her house keys from inside her workbag, enjoying their melodious jingling in the quiet of the coming evening. She raised the appropriate silver key to the large brass deadbolt and stopped. There were new scratches around the keyhole, scrapes on the metal she'd never noticed before. In truth, she couldn't exactly remember if there had ever been marks there in the past, but these just didn't look right.

Before she'd bought the house five years ago, the real estate agent had used the newly-installed security features on the country cottage as a selling point. She'd never had secure meshing on her windows when she'd lived in the city, nor external sensor lights around the porch, but they'd made the idea of living out in the sticks, all by herself, a bit more comfortable. Now, at this moment of uneasiness, she was finally grateful for them.

Ignoring the sharp icicle of trepidation that had lodged itself in her stomach, Erica inserted the key into the scratched keyhole, unlocked the deadbolt, and then the door. Once she was safely inside, she locked them again and checked them twice for good measure. In case her gut was right and those marks were new, she didn't want the person responsible to have an even easier attempt at breaking and entering.

She switched on the lights as she headed for her

bedroom, relieved as their warm glow lit up the murky shadows inside. Though she knew she was likely on edge from the constant phone calls that had been harassing her and that it was probable her deadbolt was scored when she bought the place, she couldn't shift the discomfort she felt. Things hadn't been normal, been right since she'd first slept with Matt. Even though she knew it wasn't his fault and that there was a deep part of her that wanted to keep him in her life, the part of her mind which liked to rationalize things kept coming back to his connection to all of it.

Could she have saved herself a lot of trouble if she'd just turned him down in the first place? Would he have started a relationship with someone else, encouraging the person behind the phone calls to harass some other poor woman instead? Who knew? Either way, it was too late.

Light flooded her bedroom as she flicked the switch and stepped inside. The familiar tinge of lavender in the white paint offered a soothing appeal, which helped subdue her rampant heartbeat. As an artist, she was quite eclectic in taste and it reflected in her bedroom's décor. The mahogany wood of her bookshelves, bureau, and nightstand complemented the mirrored wardrobe as well as the wine-colored curtains and the bed's duvet. While the varied artwork on the walls didn't quite clash, their principal hues of bright yellow and green pulled the eye in their direction. Novels and art reference books cluttered most surfaces and were surrounded by kitschy trinkets and photo frames featuring family and friends. Besides her shop and the workspace she'd created with the extra area in her garage, Erica's room was her sanctuary. All problems eventually seemed minor after spending time rejuvenating in there.

Sitting down on the side of the bed, she dropped the bag on the mattress beside her and rummaged through it until she found the wad of mail. Tossing a bill here, an interesting catalog there, it was a moment or two before she stumbled across something peculiar. When she pulled the envelope free of the pile, the realization that there was no postmark or stamp attached had the hair on the back of her neck standing to attention, and that stone of fear in her stomach weighing heavily. Her address had been neatly handwritten in cursive, which appeared slightly more feminine than masculine, but other than that there were no additional distinguishing marks.

Unable to stop her hands from shaking, Erica unsealed it and pulled out the thin letter within. It was a folded, crinkled sheet of paper with red text so thick it had bled onto the other side. As she opened it, the huge words written there became obvious.

STAY AWAY FROM HIM!

Erica fumbled, her fingers trembling and the letter fell to the floor.

CHAPTER 22

The red and blue flashing lights of the single squad car parked in Erica's driveway made the previously serene forestscape around her home appear lurid and ominous, as trunks and leaves alike lit up and fell dark in a flickering pattern. Matt hugged Erica close as they stood on the brightly-lit porch addressing the female police officer in front of them, while waiting for the male officer to return from his inspection inside.

"Can you think of anything else that has happened recently that might be relevant?" The mature female officer who had introduced herself as Constable Broadhurst kept her pen poised over her notepad.

Matt stared at Erica, caressing her shoulder gently until her distant expression became one of coherence. Dusky circles had formed beneath her eyes, making her appear frazzled and haunted. He'd never seen her look so vulnerable and it made his heart ache, but he'd been relieved her first instinct had been to call him. It meant a lot that she'd chosen to turn to him in her time of need.

Erica finally looked up at him. "Just the calls"—her eyes searched his—"the door and ... the letter." The last word came out croaky, her eyes falling from his for a moment as she swallowed deeply.

"Unfortunately"—Constable Broadhurst's serious tone recaptured Matt's attention—"without more to go on there's not much we can do. The calls, you say, are from an unknown number. If you surrender your phone, we can get our guys to look into it, but there's no guarantee that it will provide a connection to the letter or the damage to your front door. In reference to that, even you yourself have said you remain unsure whether the damage on your deadbolt is new or was there previously. Without proof otherwise, there isn't much we can do to prove an attempted B and E. As for the letter, we've taken it into evidence, but without more to go on, it'll likely be dismissed as no more than a prank." She paused, letting her comments settle in, flicking a look from Matt to Erica before continuing. "Any further information you believe might be related to this would be very beneficial."

Matt followed Constable Broadhurst's firm stare over to Erica, who was now wringing her hands together. She bit her bottom lip and then lifted her gaze to his.

"What about the mystery gifts you've received?" Erica asked quietly.

Matt's lips twitched. Surely, the incidents weren't related. The surprises he'd received creeped him out a little, of course, but they were in no way threatening. He was almost positive they had to be a practical joke. Even though he hadn't yet had a chance to ask Nate, it made perfect sense that his buddy would be involved with something like this. It just had to be him, not some silly secret admirer.

"Mystery gifts?" Constable Broadhurst scribbled something on her notepad. "What kind of *gifts*, sir?"

Matt shook his head and waved his hand to dismiss the question. "I'm sure it's nothing, really." As the words left his mouth, his eyes connected with Erica's, and the concern he saw there, the apprehension shadowing her stunning features had him rethinking his decision. Pulling her even closer, he kissed the top of her head affectionately. Then, he looked at the Constable. "Actually, that's not true. I don't *really* know that it's nothing."

Constable Broadhurst nodded, causing her brunette ponytail to bounce from where it had been threaded through the back of her blue police-issue cap. "Why don't you tell me, sir, and we can decide together if it might be of relevance?"

Matt sighed and then opened his mouth to explain.

Having closed Erica's front door, Matt clicked the deadbolt into place before checking his wristwatch. Their discussion with the police, which had felt more like an interrogation, had seemed to last for hours, and yet, it was still only after seven.

"Do you want me to rustle up some dinner?" He asked Erica as he headed into the kitchen. "Or I could always order in something?"

She was seated on a tall stool at the kitchen island, her elbows propped on the granite countertop, her head resting in her hands. Her attention shifted in his direction. "I don't know. I'm not very hungry, but help yourself if you are."

After Matt had relayed the antics of his secret admirer, Constable Broadhurst had convinced Erica to surrender her phone in the hopes of there being a connection to the harassing caller, the letter, and the gifts. She'd also suggested Matt bring the remaining presents to the station for testing in the morning. While neither officer had discovered enough evidence to suggest there was any immediate threat or that the threat issued was of a serious nature, the scary situation had really rattled Erica. Her home and her privacy had been violated, and it was taking its toll on her physically and emotionally.

"You should eat," he told her as he took a seat on the stool beside her.

Her eyes sparkled as she lifted her head from her palms. "Who are you? My mother?"

Pleased she wasn't so far gone as to have lost her sense of humor, Matt reached for her hand. "No, just a concerned boyfriend."

Her brow furrowed at that, but she laced her fingers through his. "As we're both exhausted and I am so entirely grateful for your being here, I'm going to let that comment slide."

Matt smiled, content that maybe just for tonight, he'd won that battle.

Erica leaned closer. "Have I thanked you yet for coming to my aid?"

"Only about a dozen times."

"Well, thank you again." She placed a chaste kiss on his lips. "I don't think I could have handled things without you."

With her hand still in his, he pulled her up from the stool and turned her, getting her to perch herself on his lap. Wrapping his arms securely around her waist, he nuzzled his face into her neck, breathing her in. Her body felt so good against his. She was so warm, so soft in all the right places, so fittingly lean and solid in others. Erica let her head fall to rest on his, her whole body relaxing into his embrace.

"I could stay like this forever."

Her quiet words surprised him, making his heartbeat quicken with the promise of hope. Matt tenderly kissed the velvety column of her neck, relishing the way she tilted her head to the side as though offering him better access. He inhaled the delectable scent of her, before lifting a hand from its position at her waist to release her hair from the clip it had been bundled up in. Her long, dark, chocolate-colored curls fell over her shoulder as he placed the clip on the counter.

"I'm always going to be here for you," he told her, his lips gently brushing her neck as he cuddled her tighter.

"Whenever you need me. You can depend on me, Erica."

At his words, she turned her head toward him and stared deep into his eyes. "I want to believe you. But, I also don't want to get hurt."

"Me, neither." Matt grinned. "So, let's just promise not to hurt each other."

He had yearned for this closeness. Every minute, every second away made him ache for her. With Erica in his arms, Matt felt as though the puzzle of the universe was complete. He'd found where he fit in life, the perfect woman he fit with, and knew with his whole heart how happy their life would be together.

"You act as though it would be so easy." She frowned at him, searching his face.

He shrugged his shoulders and pressed a brief kiss to her lips. "You're the only one who's making this hard. I know what I want and where I stand, and I won't give up until I have you permanently in my life. The timeframe, however, is up to you."

Her dark eyebrows furrowed as she swallowed uneasily. "How can you be so certain?"

Because I love you.

The thought begged to be said, but Matt held it back. Those three, little words would be a sure thing to have her reeling away out of his arms. She wasn't quite ready to hear them, and tonight, after all she'd been through, it was definitely not the night for them to be said for the first time.

Matt breathed out a sigh and rested his head on her shoulder. "Because you're everything I want," he told her. "You are incredibly passionate, you're genuine, driven, and intelligent. You're gorgeous." He glanced back at her and touched his nose to hers, before kissing her briefly. "You're kindhearted and caring. You're independent and confident in who you are. All summed up, you're irresistible to me, Erica."

As he stared deep into her mesmerizing gaze, he saw

165

tears form there like glistening diamonds. "It's the truth." Matt's chest tightened as he watched her wipe at her cheeks. "But I never meant to upset you."

Erica shook her head. "You didn't." Her eyes were reddened when they returned to his. "Just kiss me."

She captured his mouth with hers as she turned in his arms and pressed herself against him. Her lips were salty, her mouth all warm sweetness as he stood, wrapped his hands around her ass and lifted her to the countertop. She slipped her hands around his neck while their kiss continued slowly, but passionately, as though they were discovering the taste and feel of each other for the first time all over again.

When Matt lifted the hem of her gray tank top with his fingertips, Erica broke the kiss to raise her arms. He stripped it free of her and tossed it to the floor as she tugged at the buttons of his blue business shirt. Once all were unfastened, she slid her hands up his bare chest, over the smattering of brown hair covering his pecs, caressing over each contour until she reached his shoulders and forced the fabric down his arms to the tiled floor.

Matt's breath caught at the sensuality in her look, at the hunger there that seemed just for him as she stared into his eyes, her kiss-swollen lips slightly parted as though hoping for more. She was so lovely, so captivating. His heart ached to clutch her to him, to lose himself in her kiss, in her touch. She had to know what she did to him, how she made him feel. Was it so wrong of him to hope, to believe that the look in her eyes as she gazed at him was filled with true affection, with growing love? He was so certain she felt it, too. No matter how much she protested, this here, her tender expression, was his evidence to prove she truly cared for him.

When she used her fingertips to trace delicate lines from his neck to the waistband of his black slacks, Matt couldn't resist her any longer. He dipped his head, his mouth covering hers, taking her harder this time, his desire obvious and eager. Erica moaned against him as he felt the material of his trousers fall away from his hips. He barely had enough time to step free of them and kick off his shoes before she slipped her hand beneath his navy boxers and closed around the erect, solid length of him.

He groaned, his head falling back, breaking their kiss as the sensation of her stroking him, up then down, overwhelmed him momentarily. His stare had darkened hungrily, lustfully, when it returned to hers. Erica grinned at him, the same wickedly-alluring grin that had made him fall so hard for her from the very beginning.

"You have no idea, do you?" Matt asked her, his voice raspy with need. "No idea how you make me feel? Or how much I want you?"

As her eyebrow arched, he didn't give her a chance to respond. He pulled her to him, his lips going to her jaw, down her neck as her breathing quickened. He used his skilled fingers to remove her black lacy bra in seconds before popping the button on her jean shorts, then tugging them and her flimsy ebony panties over the delicious curve of her ass and down her slender legs.

She wrapped her thighs around his hips while his aching erection found her core moist and hot, as desperate for him as he was for her. She sucked the air from him when he filled her. Her mouth hungrily eating at his while their tongues caressed each other in a sensual dance. Matt growled at the sensation of her so snug around him, their bodies locking together so naturally, so marvelously. As they rocked rhythmically, he gently thrust his hips to meet hers, he held onto her tightly when she whimpered, her head lolling to the side. He kissed her throat, her collarbone, before slipping a hand up and over the delectably-plump mound of her breast, and then higher up along her neck to cup her face. Erica's dark eyes immediately fluttered open, connecting with his as she framed his face with her hands, caressing his cheeks with her thumbs.

Matt stared into those hypnotizing brown eyes, relishing in the hot, ardent look that filled them as he thrust deep inside her, filling her whole. She moaned low in her throat, a mixture of pleasurable pain and ecstasy in her gaze, before lifting her lips to meet his. Her kiss was so gentle, so tender, that his hopeful heart swelled elatedly. It wasn't just lust she felt for him, he knew that, and this once again proved it. How much longer would she try to deny it?

When she broke the kiss, she remained close, her eyes lost in the depths of his, while he continued to fill her, to press deep within her as they both climbed toward a rapturous release. As Matt watched, something flickered within those alluring eyes. A glimmer of uncertainty? A flash of apprehension? Then she brushed her lips over his but didn't quite kiss him. It was so soft like the flutter of butterfly wings, almost like the very first time she'd kissed him, but the kiss didn't deepen. Then, she spoke.

"I think I'm falling in love with you."

It was barely a whisper, not more than an exhale of breath, but Matt had heard it.

As his heart somersaulted in his chest, his mouth seized Erica's eagerly. The rhythm of their lovemaking hastened as he began to lose himself in the taste of her, in the feel of her supple curves pressed against him. While he savored every tantalizing sensation, Erica's moans rose in pitch until they became small, uncontrollable cries of desire. When their passion reached that euphoric climax, that wondrously, earthshattering explosion of absolute pleasure, another groan tore free of his throat, and he clutched her to him as she cried out blissfully.

CHAPTER 23

Erica couldn't sleep. Although her current insomnia probably had more to do with the fact that she was still unnerved by the menacing letter she'd received, she'd chosen instead to lay blame on the night's sleeping arrangements.

Earlier in the evening, after sating one desire, she and Matt had partially dressed before organizing a quick dinner of sandwiches and snack foods, before migrating to the living room. There, they had chatted in front of the television, bonding over their past as a late-night eighties comedy played out across the screen. Erica had felt so comfortable in Matt's embrace that she'd relaxed, pulling him down onto the cushions with her until they lay together, spooning on the length of her sofa. Even now, he still had his arms around her, hugging her close as he breathed steadily, lost in the realms of sleep.

She had been pleasantly surprised when he'd been content to drift off there, when he hadn't suggested they retire to her bedroom. She knew her reasons for avoiding it seemed silly, but she just wasn't ready to take that step. Her bed was sacred. She hadn't slept with a man there since her last relationship ended five long years ago. It had always felt too permanent to invite them in, as though it would cement their status as a couple and then a full-blown relationship would ensue. Limiting access to her bed was her boundary, it was how she'd kept her distance, how she'd protected her heart from emotional sabotage. It had always worked successfully—until now.

Her feelings for Matt were growing alarmingly fast, and she knew that he was quickly becoming her exception. She longed to have him in her bed, cuddling, kissing, enjoying each other. Even imagining waking up together with him, being there to kiss him good morning made her feel warm inside. She knew her heart had trapped itself in scary territory, where one wrong move could hurt her forever, and it terrified her almost as much as the threatening letter.

That thought had her desiring space. Careful not to wake him, Erica removed Matt's solid arm from her waist, crawling free to crouch on the floor beside him before replacing it back on the softness of the sofa. He grunted quietly, and his dark, handsome features contorting before he settled once more.

As she stared at him, her heart skipped a few beats. He'd only bothered to slip on his navy cotton boxers, and his bare, well-muscled chest called to her, daring her to touch him. His full lips were parted slightly as though asking to be kissed, and his rich brown hair was still tousled from where her fingers had tunneled through it while she'd lost herself in the feeling of his naked body thrusting against hers.

With a shake of her head, she pushed the thought away. She had it bad. Somehow, she'd let him get under her skin, sneak into the depths of her heart and mark himself on her soul. She adored his company, craved his touch, and worst of all, she missed him when they weren't together. What was wrong with her? She used to be so good at separating sex from her true feelings.

Rising to her feet, Erica made her way silently out of the living room and into the kitchen, hoping a cup of tea would settle her nerves. She didn't turn on the lights as she entered. The glow of the moon outside offered enough brightness as it shone through the sheer curtains over the picture window, which overlooked the front porch and gravel driveway. After switching on the kettle, she removed a large mug from the cabinet over the stove, tossing a teabag inside from a royal blue tin on the bench.

As she waited, she rested her hands on the cool granite top of the kitchen island, her mind drifting momentarily to what had happened across the counter only hours before. Apart from the gray tank top and black panties she'd put back on, the rest of her clothes and Matt's had remained there on the other side. Again, that stupid grin spread her lips as her thoughts delved into their earlier sexual adventures. Grimacing, she closed her eyes tightly. Matt had turned her into a lovesick teenager. She needed to try to keep things in perspective.

He wanted her, he wanted a relationship, but was she ready to take that leap with him? Was she prepared to give up five good years of building a happy, successful life for herself, five years of focusing on her passion, doing what she loved, to take a risk on a man she'd known for a couple of weeks? Erica rubbed her fingers over her eyelids. She didn't know the answer.

As the kettle began to bubble audibly, Erica sighed and lowered her hand from her eyes. Glancing up, her gaze drifted to the gleam of the sheer curtains and the veiled view beyond, before settling on a dark shape in her driveway. It looked like a car.

Strange, she was certain she'd left hers parked in the garage, and hadn't Matt left his Range Rover on the other side of the house to keep the way clear for when the police had arrived? That had her considering another possibility—maybe it was the police? Perhaps they'd decided to return to check on the place? But surely, if they had, they would've warned her? And it seemed odd she hadn't heard them arrive; the *crunch* of her gravel lane usually alerted her to visitors. Perhaps she'd actually dozed off in Matt's arms?

Wanting to make sense of the situation, Erica rounded the island and headed toward the window. If it was the police, then why had they parked like that, with the front of their car facing her property?

She stopped at the center of the window, where the two curtains met, then raised her hand to the edge of the silky fabric and hesitated. From this position, she could see more clearly through the misty fabric, and what she couldn't see alarmed her. The long sedan was dark in color and there appeared to be a shadowy figure at the wheel. But where were the red and blue emergency lights which usually sat atop a police vehicle? Could it be possible this was an unmarked car? She very much doubted it. If Constable Broadhurst and her partner hadn't believed they'd received enough evidence to create a legitimate case, then Erica doubted they'd spare the resources to send anything more than a squad car.

Her pulse quickened as her stomach roiled. If the sedan didn't belong to the police, then who was sitting in the driver's seat? She gasped as weighty fear, heavy like an anvil, dropped into her gut. Was this the person who'd sent her the letter? The same person who'd warned her to stay away from Matt only to find her with him once more?

Erica swallowed back the urge to scream. She had to contain herself. Calling for Matt wouldn't help the situation. She had an opportunity to see this person, a chance to look out the window and find out who they were. If she did, she could turn them in, and this madness would end. All she needed to do was peel back the curtain enough to get an unobstructed view outside. She could do that; she was strong enough to do that.

Fighting against fear's frozen hold, Erica forced herself to reach out that final inch, her shaky fingers finally clutching around the edge of the sheer fabric. She moved slowly, carefully pulling it away from the glass. A little bit farther, and she would be able to peer clearly outside. Her whole body was shivering, trembling as she moved that last inch.

Then, with a blinding flash, the car's headlights snapped on. The penetrating brightness pierced painfully into Erica's eyes as the entire kitchen around her illuminated with warm yellow light—and she screamed.

She heard the thumping of hurried footsteps running into the kitchen, coming up beside her as her vision returned.

"Erica? What is it? Are you okay?"

Matt hugged his strong arms around her shoulders as she blinked away the intense speckles still scalding her vision.

"You're shaking? What happen ..." The word trailed off as the blaze of light in the kitchen began to subside and the eerie *crunch* of gravel filled the otherwise quiet night.

As she pushed free of his arms, wanting to show him, not sure she could find the words to tell him, Erica noticed Matt's attention had already drifted outside.

"There's a car out there," he whispered.

She nodded automatically, watching the vehicle reverse unhurriedly back up her driveway as the glow of the headlights finally drifted out of the kitchen returning it to darkness. Matt yanked back the curtain and stared through the pristine glass, his brows furrowing, eyes squinting as though he was trying to see more clearly but couldn't. Even in the moonlit night, the car remained barely visible, the encircling gleam of its headlights protecting it from view.

It had almost disappeared around the bend, sheltered even more so by the tall, bushy trees that now lined the rest of the lane back to the road, when Matt faced her again.

"Stay here," he ordered, and then he was running out of the room.

She could hear him unlocking the deadbolt, then the

front door, before she heard his bare footsteps *thud* on the wooden porch, then down the front steps. Frozen in place, her hands still trembling, Erica saw him come into view, the moonlight now the only thing illumining his muscular, half-naked figure. He ran swiftly along the rough gravel of the driveway, as though he were completely undaunted by the sharp, coarse feel of it beneath his bare feet. When he vanished around the bend, Erica's whole body went cold, her skin prickling.

What if he caught up with the car? What would happen? What if the driver had a weapon?

"Oh God." Her breath was coming in quick, sharp bursts.

She had to do something. She had to get help. Erica glanced around, flailing, fingers trembling as she tried to think. Matt's mobile phone, she could call the police. She searched around the kitchen. Where had he left it? Sprinting for the entry, she headed toward the living room but stopped before she got there. No, it wasn't on the coffee table. She peered down the hall. Her bedroom. That's right, he'd asked to put his phone to charge before dinner. Running into her room, she snatched the phone from the nightstand, ripping out the charging cord, before hurrying back down the hall. As she re-entered the kitchen she'd already dialed and pressed the phone to her ear. She was back at the window, peering out, urgently looking for Matt, when the call connected.

"You have dialed the emergency hotline," a female operator told her. "Does your emergency require an ambulance, fire and rescue, or the police?"

"Police," Erica yelled, her eyes hot with welling tears. "Police!"

Once the operator had transferred her, Erica relayed her address and the situation to the mature-sounding gentleman on the other end of the line, ensuring she mentioned Constable Broadhurst and her earlier report. When he asked whether or not she wanted to stay on the line until the police arrived, Erica spotted Matt jogging back around the bend, his half-naked form glowing angelically in the moonlight.

"He's back," she said, her limbs tingling at the sight of him, making her feel suddenly lightheaded. "No, no. He's okay. He's back."

Turning away from the window, she ended the call, tossing the phone on the island's countertop, before dashing into the entry and flinging open the front door.

"Matt!" She called out to him as she darted over the threshold and down the stairs.

He ran faster when he saw her, reaching her as her bare feet met the harsh gravel. She threw herself at him, slipping her arms around his neck, clutching him to her as he slid his hands around her waist. She kissed his mouth, his cheek, his mouth again as tears trickled down her face.

"I'm okay," he told her, once she'd calmed enough to stop and just hold him. "I'm okay."

Her racing heartbeat slowed at his words, at the feel of his strong, muscular body safely in her arms.

"I know." She blinked back another tear before wiping at her eyes.

"Come on." His voice was gentle, coaxing. "Let's go inside. I should call the police."

"I already have." She pulled back from him, looking up into his eyes. "They're on their way."

"Good." He nodded as he steered her back toward the house. "I didn't get the number plate, but I'm pretty sure I know what model it was."

Erica gripped his hand tightly in hers, her legs jittery and unstable as they climbed the front stairs. "Do you think ..." Her voice cracked, and she glanced up at him as she swallowed against a painful dryness in her throat. "How long do you think they were out there?" Stopping his stride on the porch, Matt turned his sunken gaze to her before looking back over his shoulder at the empty driveway. As Erica did the same, the eerie memory of the car and its driver lurking there, watching them, haunted her. An icy shiver shook her as the hair on the back of her neck stood on end.

When Matt's dark eyes returned to hers, his pursed lips and furrowed brow said it all.

"I don't know," he told her. "I just don't know."

CHAPTER 24

"Do the police have any suspects?"

Nate hadn't touched his homemade pasta primavera since *the stalker* had become the topic of their lunchtime conversation. His zealous expression had Matt wondering if his friend was enjoying their discussion a little too much.

"Not that I've heard." Matt rubbed the back of his hand over his sore, tired eyes. "Apparently there are several vehicles in town which match the description. So, they're focusing on trying to trace the call, but that will take some time." His heart felt weighty in his chest, his limbs even heavier as he poked a fork at the remainder of his salad.

As usual, they were having their break in the cozy office kitchen, one of the only rooms, besides the bathroom, that had been entirely remodeled and refurbished in the turn-of-the-century house turned medical practice. Most days they were joined by Melina, but she'd had plans to meet with Jocelyn today. Her absence, and therefore the lack of a direct line to the gossip circle in town, had made Nate decidedly chatty.

"So, what? You're just going to sit around and wait, hoping they'll pull their fingers out of their asses and find the guy? What if he comes after Erica again?" Nate's indignance attracted Matt's attention.

"It hasn't even been twelve hours, buddy." Matt sighed. "And the police have already suggested Erica not be left alone until the matter is resolved. That's why Melina is meeting Jocelyn at Unique Art Boutique instead of the café. Jocelyn has agreed to stay with Erica for the day."

Matt covered his mouth as he yawned. Neither he nor Erica had slept much after the incident. Besides spending time giving their statements to the police, including the detective placed on the case, Detective Senior Constable Walsh, they had also found themselves suffering from fear-induced insomnia. While Erica was afraid that their uninvited visitor might return, Matt was more concerned by the thought of anything horrible happening to the woman he loved.

He was still severely disturbed by morbid nightmares of what might have happened had Erica's scream not woken him. He had chided her when she'd told him that she hadn't roused him, because she'd believed there wasn't much more he could do. Even though he understood her reasoning, that she could glance out the window just as well as he could, he would much rather have been there, awake next to her, protecting her, than asleep, blissfully unaware of the danger that might harm her.

"I still think we should do something," Nate grumbled.

"I wish there was something we could do."

"There is, mate."

"Okay then, enlighten me."

Nate grinned. "I'm good at lists, remember?"

Immediately Matt's thoughts went to the night he'd received cupcakes from his secret admirer—now very possibly Erica's stalker—and he reflected back to the notes Nate had compiled. "You want to make a list of potential suspects?"

"Exactly. We can include anyone and everyone who has a connection to the two of you and then narrow it down. I had assumed your secret admirer was female, but now that the two incidents might be connected, I think it's time we cover all bases."

Matt stared hard at Nate as he pondered over the proposition. It wasn't the worst idea Nate had had in his lifetime. Even the police had asked them if they knew of anyone acting suspiciously of late, encouraging them to suggest everyone they believed could have been involved. Since neither of them had been able to think of particular individuals, Erica had offered to provide the police with a list of attendees to her life drawing class. At the time, Matt had been disappointed he hadn't been able to assist further, but perhaps with Nate's help, he could.

"Okay." Matt drew the word out slowly.

Nate's eyes widened. "Okay?"

Matt nodded. "Yes. I think it's a good idea. Let's do it."

*

"Thanks for walking me, Seels." Erica smiled over at her best friend before locking the front door to Unique Art Boutique. "Matt should be at my place by now, so I'll be fine to do the drive home alone."

"Are you sure?"

"Yeah." Erica double-checked that the store's entry was secure, then triple-checked it for good measure. "I don't need a babysitter in a locked car."

"Okay, well …" Seeley gnawed at her lower lip as they headed down the cobblestone path to the parking lot. "Maybe I'll follow you in my car, see that you get home safely. You know Matt would kill me if anything happened to you."

"Fine, Seels. Do what you need to do."

They followed the curve in the path which led down a charming, tree-lined avenue, made all the more picturesque by the glow of the late afternoon sun. From this short distance, Erica could see her little red hatchback was one of only a few cars remaining in the gravel parking lot. While it had never bothered her before, it unnerved her now to see it parked all alone with such a great deal of space between it and the others. With what she'd been through recently, the sparse placement seemed to lend itself to all sorts of frightening possibilities, and she was once again very grateful for her friend's company.

"So, how are things between the two of you then?" Seeley's tense posture eased as her hands slipped into the pockets of her black skinny jeans. "Getting along?"

Erica swallowed and grabbed the strap of her paisley workbag, lifting it higher on her shoulder over the cotton of her cherry-red blouse. "Yes. Of course, we're getting along well."

"*Very* well from what I hear."

"Don't believe everything you hear through the town's grapevine."

Seeley smirked. "I heard he's been sleeping in your bed."

Erica's jaw fell. Now that really was a lie. While she could no longer pretend she didn't want him there, they were yet to take that final leap into a committed, monogamous relationship. Erica still didn't think she was ready, but she was ready for him. She wanted Matt, needed him, and that's all that really counted.

She glowered at her best friend. "Well, has Tom been sleeping in *your* bed?"

Glaring right back, Seeley poked out her tongue. "Touché."

Erica laughed. "See what cheekiness gets you?"

As they neared her car, Erica rummaged through her shoulder bag for her keys, clicking the unlocking mechanism once she'd found them. The car's lights flashed briefly before she opened the driver's side door. After tossing her bag across to the passenger's seat, Erica turned back to Seeley, who was still hovering behind her.

"Good to go?" She noticed the frown-lines creasing her

friend's forehead. "Or not?"

"Sure," Seeley nodded. "I'm still going to be your one-woman motorcade, but I've just got to ask, Erica … are you still planning to go ahead with the life drawing class tomorrow?"

Erica's eyes lit up. Of all possible questions, she hadn't been expecting that. "Definitely. I'm not going to let anyone scare me away from doing what I love."

"I know. I'm with you," Seeley told her. "It's just … what if your stalker shows up there? What if it's someone already in the class?"

Erica rested her arm on the cool metal of the car door frame. "Then we'll deal with it, Seels. Besides, the fact that the police now have the entire list of names of all class members to help them narrow down a suspect list, you'll also be there. Matt and Nate will be there. Even Tonya has told me she'll be coming again. I won't be alone. I'm not going to cancel a class when thirty people are counting on me to run it, not even if one of them happens to be my suspected stalker."

Seeley's brows knit, so Erica reached out and took her hand.

"It will be fine, Seels," she said. "Really."

Unlike many of the other things in her present circumstances, her safety at the life drawing class was something Erica felt almost one hundred percent confident about. She sincerely doubted her stalker would try anything in front of so many people. It was those times when she was completely alone that she worried about, like going into the storeroom at work or taking a long, hot shower, or driving home alone. Her terrified imagination ran away with her, creating horrifying situations every time she closed her eyes.

As a shiver tickled along her spine, Erica released Seeley's hand and then faked a casual glance toward the back of her car. Her gaze went straight to the back seat, to the *empty* back seat, and she breathed a silent sigh.

With a feigned smile plastered to her face, Erica looked back at Seeley. "Shall we go?"

CHAPTER 25

"I am so sorry, Erica." Matt's head hung low as he mixed the greens with the large salad servers. "I tried. I really did. I told Nate it was a no, but then they showed up here after work and he wouldn't leave." Matt looked up at her, his handsome hazel eyes pained as he grimaced. "Honestly, I tried."

"I believe you." She rubbed his shoulder for an instant. "It's okay. I'm just tired, but with everything going on, more company is probably a good thing."

"I guess. I would have preferred to warn you though, but with the police still having your phone, there wasn't much I could do before you arrived home." He stopped mixing and raised a hand to rub it over his eyes and down his cheek. "Then I saw Seeley's face in the car behind you. She just stared at us all as we waited on the porch, looking like she'd just seen Hell."

Erica chuckled. "I don't think she could imagine anything worse than a social call from Nate and Tonya."

Matt reached for her, pulling her away from where she'd laid the final portion of oven-baked salmon on the last individual plate. He wrapped his arms around her waist before dipping his head to kiss her softly.

"I'm sorry my best buddy's a bossy bastard and that I don't yet have the crass wit and rigorous tactlessness to tell him to push off when he's standing there in front of his new girlfriend."

With a giggle, Erica kissed him back. "As long as they've got no plans to stay the night with us, your apology is well and truly accepted."

"Thank God," he breathed, and then his mouth met hers again, more passionately this time.

She relaxed against him, taking comfort in his solid embrace as he held her tightly, pressing the line of his strong body to hers. This is what home should really feel like, Erica realized as her heart swelled contentedly. This feeling seemed much more important than the need to retain her bed as a boundary, as a form of both privacy and protection. What she experienced in Matt's arms, the compassion, the tenderness, the genuine love felt as though it were enough for her to break down the last of her barriers and risk it all. Maybe it was finally time?

"Erica, hon, Nate's going wild over your superior movie collection—oh, whoops, I'm clearly interrupting."

Erica and Matt broke their kiss abruptly to glance over in Tonya's direction. Even after her own admission, Tonya didn't make a move to leave from where she'd entered the kitchen. She just stood there in the doorway, looking provocative as usual in her black mini-skirt and baby blue blouse, a grin spreading her pink painted lips.

"We're going to have a ball on Saturday choosing one," she continued. "I don't know what the other girls will vote for, but I'm partial to a raunchy romance. Do you think you might have one?" She winked at them playfully.

From the corner of her eye, Erica saw Matt cast an amused expression in her direction, but kept her gaze fixed to Tonya's instead. "How about I write you a list," Erica offered.

"On the topic of lists," Nate said, entering the room from the entry behind Tonya, "Matt and I have made one of our own."

"Matt's been telling me," Erica said, gesturing for Matt to take the salad to the small, neatly laid dining table at the far end of the room. She followed behind him with two plates of salmon, nodding her silent thanks to Tonya when she picked up the other two. "I've heard you've narrowed it down to a final five."

Matt placed the salad beside a bread basket, then took his seat as Erica and Tonya laid the individual plates on the table and did the same.

"Yes, five potentials," Nate agreed, taking his seat beside Tonya, opposite their hosts. "Although, we were hoping you might add your input."

"Me?" Erica let out a hoot in disbelief. "I've already given the police and you two junior detectives a list of attendees to the life drawing class. Since the phone calls began the morning after and I'd never had a problem before, I thought that was the best bet."

When her brows creased, Matt quickly took her hand in his, resting both on top of the table before caressing the back of hers with his thumb.

"We wondered," Matt suggested, "if it might be helpful for us to consider a few of your more recent relationships. Basically," he swallowed, "a couple of your exes."

Since it was common knowledge that her last relationship ended before she'd arrived in town over five years ago, Erica bit back another laugh. "I'm not trying to discount your idea, but I don't really understand the point. I haven't seen any of them in years, and as for anyone in the interim, we've never stayed in touch." She shrugged, wishing she could offer them something useful as it was obvious they had the best of intentions. "Besides Matt," she beamed at him before looking across the table at Nate, "there hasn't been anyone in my life in *that* way for a very long time."

Erica felt Matt's hand squeeze hers lightly as though acknowledging the enormity of what she'd just admitted.

"It was worth a try." Nate sighed. "It's only that our list doesn't include any *men*. And, both of us"—he pointed an index finger at Matt—"considered that pretty strange."

*

"I can't believe you're letting me do this," Matt said, the exhilaration bubbling in his voice resembling that of a little kid at Christmas.

"Calm yourself," Erica ordered, she poised her hand on the door handle to her bedroom. "And stop reminding me of how big a deal this is, or I might decide to retract my offer."

Matt's stomach had been in excited knots ever since Erica had whispered in his ear after dinner, telling him that he'd be sleeping in her room tonight. He had been fidgety all through the action movie the four of them had watched together, barely able to wait until they could finally farewell Nate and Tonya for the night.

It was a huge step for her, a massive stride for them as a couple. Erica was actually willing to bring her barrier down for him, removing the last obstacle between them, and Matt was utterly ecstatic. Although she hadn't quite verbalized it, he knew what this meant, what this signified for her. She was letting him in completely, accepting him into her life, finally agreeing—in not so many words—that they were in a relationship. She was proving she truly loved him, just as he had loved her since the day they had met.

Matt gazed at her, grinning like an idiot, his heart racing as he waited for her to open the door.

"Ready?" She asked him, sounding as though she was checking her own position rather than his.

He nodded. "I'm ready, I'm calm."

She narrowed her eyes at him, but then conceded and opened the door. Matt peered into the large room, taking in the off-white walls hinted with lavender, the bright summery artwork, and the charming clutter of knickknacks and personal mementos. The mahogany of her furniture and the wine-colored curtains and duvet gave the otherwise-cheerful room a tinge of sensual warmth. It was no wonder Erica had wanted to keep the room private, it was like a piece of her, revealing visually the little idiosyncrasies and traits of her personality that made her who she was—the woman he loved.

"It's beautiful," he told her, "exactly like you." Then he dashed into the room, hurrying over to the bed. He threw his body onto it like a big kid, laying down with a bounce on the cushy duvet. Then he patted the empty side next to him. "You coming?"

She frowned at him from the doorway. "Don't make me regret inviting you in."

"It's too late to take it back," he chortled. "Come join me, and I'll make it all better."

Erica raised an eyebrow but did as he suggested. She climbed on the bed, curling up beside him, her head resting on his shoulder as he cuddled his arm around her. A deep sigh escaped his lips at the contentment that filled him. He could imagine doing this forever, snuggled close to Erica, together in their own bed, in their own home. Could there have been anything better?

"Why did you have to be so bloody perfect?" It left her lips as a grumble. "My life was fine before you came along, and then you had to show me how much better it could be."

"I didn't want you missing out."

"Smartass." She lifted the hand she'd laid across his chest to draw circles over the fabric of his ivory business shirt.

The ticklish feeling of her finger stroking him stirred his hunger for her. Slipping his hand from her shoulder, he caressed the curve of her waist, over the soft cotton of her red blouse, and down to the waistband of her black shorts at her hip. He felt her head turn on his chest, and he glanced down at her, catching her gorgeous eyes. The look she gave him was so adoring, so sincere.

"I think you're the first man in my life who hasn't run away when things started to get tough."

Matt's heart ached. The reverence and honesty in her words touched him deeply. It infuriated him that those she'd loved in the past had dared to leave her in her time of need. Even though they'd discussed brief details about her failed relationships, she'd never wanted to dwell on them, never wanted to let them impact what they shared together. In that moment, Matt thought Erica's restraint in discussing them made those men very lucky assholes. They'd never deserved her, still didn't deserve her discretion, and yet, she battled through them, through her past, to focus on the happiness she wanted in her present, in her future.

"Even though it terrifies me," Erica continued, "even though I doubt my heart will heal if you ever break it, I need you to know, Matt, that I am"—as her voice quivered, she paused briefly—"so desperately in love with you."

Matt thought his heart might burst from his chest. He felt suddenly light, weightless even, as though his body might lift up from the mattress, levitating there above the world.

He hadn't counted what she'd said to him the other night during their passionate embrace. He'd wanted her to be sure of her feelings for him before he revealed his own, yet he still hadn't expected that she would be the one to so openly declare her love first. It was so incredible, so mind-blowing, it left him lost for words.

Erica loved him. Erica *loved* him. It was all he had wanted since the day he'd met her.

He grasped her around the waist, lifting her on top of him, her legs straddling his jean-clad hips, before enveloping her in his arms again and pulling her chest down to meet his. He raised his head slightly, pressing his lips to hers, devouring her in an ardent kiss as her supple figure relaxed. She tasted sweet, smelled even better, and the curves of her body were deliciously warm as they fit flawlessly along the line of his.

As she moaned and pressed the delta of her thighs harder against his aching groin, Matt broke the kiss, but only for an instant, only long enough to tell her what he'd yearned to express since meeting her.

"I love you, Erica," he growled. "I love you more than anything, and I will never let you down."

TAMMY MANNERSLY

CHAPTER 26

The classroom at Unique Art Boutique was full to capacity for the weekly life drawing session. Erica had even let a couple of stragglers, those people who hadn't booked but had begged to join, take a seat on the floor on whatever cushions or blankets she could provide. In spite of the ruckus the thirty-five or so people created as they mingled with each other, chatting before class, now seemingly more interested in the social aspect and the lesson itself than the novelty of the men, Erica was more than grateful for the large crowd. More people meant more protection or more witnesses should something untoward happen if her stalker really was among them.

While setting up for the event, Matt and Erica had agreed that at no point during the night's proceedings should she ever be left alone with any of the attendees. Seeley, Nate, and Tonya had also offered their assistance, promising that Matt or one of them would be by her side at all times throughout the evening. Knowing they had her back, that they would be there keeping a watchful eye over anyone or anything suspicious, had let Erica relax into the normalcy of the classroom atmosphere, so much that at brief moments she completely forgot the reasons she had to be afraid.

"Single white female at two o'clock," Tonya whispered, taking her current posting at Erica's side rather seriously.

Following the younger blonde woman's gaze to the room's entry where the final few students were arriving, Erica saw Lauren and Diana approaching them. While Diana's eyes shifted from side to side, taking in the sizeable gathering, Lauren smiled, her gaze focused on them as she neared. She held a semitransparent plastic container in her hands, which when paired with her pretty pink sundress, made her appear all the more like a sweet, wannabe housewife. Diana on the other hand, in her casual blue jeans and plain navy blouse, provided a stark contrast.

"Hi, ladies." Erica returned Lauren's smile as the two women stopped in front of them. "How are we doing tonight?"

"Happy to be here." Lauren lifted the container toward Erica.

Erica froze. "What's this?"

To her surprise, a cold tingling crept down her back, even though she could clearly see the object inside was a baked good of some kind and not something worth fretting over. It seemed absurd to be fearful, but she'd been conditioned to be of late.

As though noticing her hesitation, Tonya reached for the container instead. "You can give it to me, hon. Erica's got a lot on her plate at the moment, but I can add it to the treats and nibbles other people have brought in."

Tonya nodded in the direction of a workbench against the far wall that was quickly becoming known as the snack table. Although it wasn't commonplace for there to be food in the classroom, since Nate and Matt's first lesson, a few of the women had begun bringing in homemade and packet-bought goodies for the students to share.

When Tonya's fingers settled on the plastic container, Lauren snatched it free again.

"No." The shrillness of Lauren's voice drew Diana's

gaze.

It took a few seconds for Tonya to lower her hands. "Okay," she snapped. "You can keep it."

"No." Lauren shook her head. "No, sorry, that's not what I meant." She stared back up at both of them, her emerald eyes wide as she tittered. "I only meant that I made this especially for Erica and her alone." She stretched the box out to Erica. "I heard about what happened. I was worried about you and didn't know how to help, so I made this."

Erica looked from Lauren, down to the container, before glancing at Tonya again, seeking confirmation. When Tonya finally shrugged, Erica reached for the gift.

"Thanks, Lauren." The large box was weighty in her hands. "You didn't have to, but thank you."

"No problem." Lauren grinned. "I like to bake. It's an apple raspberry almond cake, and remember"—she stretched out a hand, touching Erica's elbow gently as she winked—"it's all yours, so there's no need to share."

"I'll keep that in mind."

Diana appeared tense as she watched the exchange, and then, as though noticing something of interest behind them, she grabbed Lauren's arm and began pulling her away. "Come on, Lauren. There's only a couple of seats left near Dr. Garrick. I don't want to miss out." As the frantic words left Diana's lips, her gaze connected with Erica's. Blushing, she pulled Lauren away, off into the crowd of people behind them.

Erica and Tonya turned, observing the two women as they made a beeline for Matt, taking seats as close as possible, before trying to get his attention.

Tonya inhaled sharply, creating a hissing sound. "There's definitely a screw loose in that one."

"Who? Lauren?"

Tonya's mouth fell open. "No," she shook her head abruptly. "Diana. That's why she's at the top of Nate and Matt's list. She's got a dark side, and I don't think anyone really knows what's going on up inside there." She tapped her own head at her temple for emphasis.

Nodding, Erica eyed the two women who were now making flirtatious eyes at her man. Even though they were certainly not the only ones to do so, Erica had to wonder if maybe Nate and Tonya had a point about Diana. Erica had never been the best judge of character, she only had to recall her earlier track record with men to prove that. So, why couldn't she be wrong about Diana, as well? Maybe she wasn't the shy, girl-next-door type Erica had originally thought she was? But could she really be so desperate that she'd dabble in stalking?

Turning her attention back to Tonya, Erica raised the heavy plastic container toward her. "What should I do about this?"

Tonya leaned close to her. "If I were you, I'd throw it in the trash."

Erica's brown eyes widened. She'd been expecting something about how best to keep the cake fresh or where to leave it for the duration of the lesson. She hadn't considered Tonya would recommend disposing of it.

Tonya faced her, moving her body between Erica and Lauren's line of sight. "Look, hon," she kept her voice hushed. "I love Lauren, she's a sweetheart, and I'm sure she means well, but no one has been keen to eat her food since the lingerie party debacle."

"What? The one that made Yasmin and my other models sick a couple of weeks ago?"

Tonya frowned. "She's usually such a good little cook. She really knows how to use food to win people over, but it only takes one bout of food poisoning for everyone to toss your cupcakes, if you know what I mean."

Nodding, Erica stared back down at the container. "So, I should definitely bin it then?"

Tonya reached up to place a hand on Erica's shoulder. "I get that you don't want to hurt her feelings, hon, so just chuck the cake, wash the box and hand it back to her with plenty of white-lies about how scrumptious it was. It'll all be for the best, you'll see."

Erica speculated over Tonya's definition of a white-lie as Seeley's authoritative voice burst tersely from the front of the room.

"Time to settle and take your seats, people. Class is about to begin."

CHAPTER 27

"See you tomorrow for movie night." Tonya linked an arm through Nate's and dragged him toward the well-lit street as he beamed over his shoulder at Matt and Erica.

"What have I gotten myself into?" Erica glanced up at Matt's kind eyes.

"You know, I can always stick around tomorrow, if you want me to?"

She shook her head. "Having a man there kind of defeats the purpose of a girls' night, but thanks anyway."

Matt grinned at that, slipping his muscular arm through hers before leading her down the dimly-lit cobblestone path beside Unique Art Boutique, toward the parking lot.

They had just finished tidying and locking up after the long night. Although Seeley had offered to stay back and help the four of them clean, Erica had once again noticed her best friend's interest in her chirruping phone and quickly put two and two together. Sweet, shy, science teacher Tom was doing his best to make time with Seeley, and, strange as it was, her friend was just as keen. It had taken some serious convincing and some literal prodding, but Seeley had eventually conceded, relinquishing her post as one of Erica's four protectors to instead go out on another date.

It seemed a few people in town were coupling up as of late. Erica smiled as she mused over Nate and Tonya's budding relationship.

"I wasn't sure before," she said, briefly gazing up at Matt while they walked, "but now I think Tonya and Nate are well-suited. Don't you?"

"Maybe," Matt answered, "if by well-suited you're suggesting they are both as conceited as each other, then yes."

Erica chuckled. "Pardon?"

"I mean that in the most respectful way, of course." He winked. "Nate's my good friend, but it takes a special kind of person of a similar nature to accept someone's narcissistic tendencies when they affect a romantic relationship. Their similarities likely give them more insight and understanding."

"Okay, good save there, Mr. Eloquent."

Matt pulled her closer so he could kiss her cheek. "It's how I know that we're so well-suited."

Her jaw dropped. "Because of our mutual narcissism?"

Matt's shoulders shook as he whooped with laughter. "No, because of our shared compassion and need to be accepted and loved for who we truly are."

Erica's whole body warmed with his words, her heart filling with a cozy, fuzzy feeling that spread a ridiculously happy expression across her face. She wanted to kiss him breathless for those beautiful words. God, she longed to do so much more, it was as though his sentiments had set her on fire. If he was trying to seduce her right there on the public street, he was succeeding.

She was on the verge of stopping their stride, considering the idea of shoving him up against the nearest tree and ravishing him, when Diana stepped out of the shadows and onto the path. Erica jumped, flinching backward, almost stumbling over her own feet before clutching at Matt's strong arm still linked through hers.

After helping her regain her balance, Matt unlinked his arm and cuddled it around her instead.

"Sorry," Diana squeaked. "I didn't mean to scare you."

"What are you doing lurking back here?" Matt growled out the words, making Erica remember that he, too, had Diana at number one on his potential stalker list.

Diana was close to tears as she lowered her gaze from Matt's and then looked to Erica. The young woman's distress appeared so real that Erica felt for her. Could she really be capable of anything menacing when she was about to cry after a few harsh words from Matt? It didn't seem likely.

"It's okay, Diana," Erica told her, taking a deep breath to calm her racing heartbeat. "Were you waiting to talk to us?"

Grimacing, Diana wrung her hands together. "I had a really good time tonight, Erica. I wanted to tell you that."

"Thank you, Diana. That's really sweet."

A number of women from tonight's class had offered Erica positive comments about the still-life she'd arranged for them to draw. She'd chosen an old dressmaker's mannequin cloaked in flowing folds of fabric and topped with a decorative formal hat, trimmed with flowers and feathers, and it had been a crowd favorite. Most of the women in the class had thoroughly enjoyed drawing something so simple, but so feminine, and being able to focus on shadow and detail where they felt it necessary. The feedback had been so encouraging in fact, that Erica believed she'd still retain some of the newer students even after the men ceased attending.

Diana was smiling at her. It was only a small smile, but it was enough to have pushed her tears away, lightening her attractive features. Then she turned her wide eyes back to Matt and something heavy dropped in Erica's stomach.

"Dr. Garrick, would it be okay for me to talk to you alone for a moment?"

Matt's expression hardened, then he swallowed and

squared his shoulders. "I'm sorry, Diana, but I'm not comfortable leaving Erica alone right now. I'm sure whatever you need to get off your chest, you can say in front of us both."

Diana nibbled at her lower lip and cast a glance in Erica's direction, before her gaze settled once more on Matt. As she stared up at him, her mouth began to quiver and her eyes welled with tears. "What's wrong with me?" The words were barely audible, but the pain in them cut deeply.

"Diana—" Erica reached for the slightly younger woman, but Matt held her back.

"What do you mean, Diana?" He asked.

As her shoulders shook with silent sobs, tears slid down her face, but she brushed them away quickly. "I d-don't mean any d-disrespect to either of you." It came out raspy as she hiccupped with each sob. "I can tell you're happy together, but I just need to know."

"Know what?" Erica could feel Diana's pain but didn't know how to help. All she wanted was to hug the poor girl until she calmed down, to make her feel better, but Matt's tight hold on her shoulders remained unwavering.

Diana's reddened gaze rose to Matt's. "What's wrong with me?" She asked again. "Maybe if I can find out, if I can change, then someone will finally choose me?"

Realization struck Erica like lightning. Diana believed she was unlovable. She imagined there was something wrong with her and that was why she hadn't found love. It was a notion Erica completely understood. When her ex-lovers had let her down, had cheated on her, betrayed her, she'd always dragged the blame back to herself, lumping it there like a painful anvil, taking all of the responsibility for the relationship's failure. It was only once she'd recognized that nothing she could have done would have changed her ex-partners' choices or behavior, that she was finally able to cut herself free from the hefty guilt that suffocated her.

Erica was about to yank herself free of Matt's hold in

order to comfort Diana, when Matt took the opportunity to do it first. He embraced the shorter woman as though she were a child, an arm around her shoulders, while one hand clasped her head to his chest. Although muffled against the material of his slate gray shirt, Diana's sobs became more violent, shaking her whole body as the emotion fought for release.

"There is nothing wrong with you, Diana," Matt crooned to her as her sorrowful weeping pierced the quiet night air. "There never has been. The right person will love you as you are. You have to realize that. You have to wait for that."

"B-but," Diana stuttered, "what if it never happens?"

"It will," Erica told her, stepping beside them to rub Diana's back. "You just need to have faith and stop putting your life on hold. If you can find your passion, your happiness, live your life doing something you love, being a better, happier person because of it, then the right person will find you."

Diana stared at her with red, glassy eyes. "Do you really believe that?" She pulled free of Matt's embrace, searching Erica's face intently.

"I really do."

Matt rested a hand on Diana's shoulder. "So do I, Diana."

She looked from Erica to Matt and back again. "Will you help me?"

Erica glanced over at Matt, meeting his eyes. She didn't know what they could offer the poor girl besides friendship and compassion, but she nodded anyway. Maybe that was enough? Maybe Diana needed someone to encourage her, to show her what she was capable of?

The thought made Erica consider Lauren. Seeley had said the two women had been close most of their lives. Surely Lauren would be the best person for Diana to turn to in this time of depression and self-doubt. It seemed strange that Diana had chosen to open up to them in this way, but even stranger that Lauren wasn't here with her now, when they were almost always together.

Erica peered around. "Is Lauren somewhere nearby, Diana? Is she waiting for you?"

Diana shook her head. "She said she had something important to do."

"But, she's your best friend," Erica continued, "have you told her any of this? How you feel? I'm sure she'd want to help you as well."

Diana's teary eyes widened. "I can't tell Lauren." She shook her head swiftly. "She wouldn't understand."

Frowning, Erica shared another look with Matt. She understood the fear in Diana's eyes. It was terribly hard to open up, and sometimes opening up to those closest to you, those people who could be the most critical or who could have you up on a pedestal, was more terrifying than anything.

*

Matt shifted his weight in the bed, the arm he had wrapped around Erica holding her that little bit tighter. He stared up at the white ceiling of her bedroom, at the serene shadows in the dark space, and tried his best to soothe his troubled mind. But it was no good. His chest was tense; his stomach continued to pain. No matter what he did, he couldn't shake the unnerving feeling he had.

After he and Erica had walked Diana to the parking lot, ensuring she had settled enough to drive, a disturbing thought had hit him. While he'd empathized with Diana, believed her tears and pain were genuine, a little seed of doubt had sprouted when he'd seen Diana's black sedan. That doubt had grown even greater when he'd realized that the make and model of the car had matched the vehicle which had been parked in front of Erica's house a few nights ago, the same one he'd chased after while trying to get the number plate.

It could have been a coincidence. After everything that had happened tonight, it would've made perfect sense to eliminate Diana from their list of suspects, wouldn't it? She didn't seem to be emotionally or mentally stable enough to be planning threatening letters or an attempted break and entry. She would probably melt into a pool of tears, like she had tonight, if she had to do anything of the sort.

Again, that stab of doubt niggled at him, growing stronger with each moment, with each rationalizing thought. Perhaps Diana had only wanted them to believe that she was so insecure? Maybe she'd wanted them off-guard and unsure? She'd packed so much vulnerability and innocence into her behavior tonight. Who would be ruthless enough to question someone so down on themselves, so profoundly self-doubting and faint-hearted? You would have to be an outright asshole.

Still, it had been so sincere. Maybe he was overthinking things, grasping for answers because he had none.

Sighing deeply, Matt tried to ignore the unease churning in his gut. He probably just needed to sleep on it. Things would be different—better—in the morning.

He glanced down at Erica, at where she rested her head on his chest. Her face was so peaceful, her attractive features so exquisite in contented sleep. As he gazed at her, his heart seemed to stop beating, his breath catching in his throat as he stared, completely captivated. It wasn't just her beauty that had him in awe, it was her love for him, so evident in her expression, in her embrace. It was everything he'd wanted, everything he'd longed for, and everything he feared to lose.

Taking a breath, his heartbeat returning, quickening with fear, Matt realized what he needed to do. He and Nate had put it off long enough. They were doing no good keeping it to themselves, waiting, trying to perfect it further. It was finally time.

Tomorrow morning, Matt would take their list of potential suspects to the police—and Diana's name would remain securely at the top.

CHAPTER 28

"Seeley's here," Erica announced through the house as she headed for her front door.

She'd almost finished cleaning the living room when she'd heard the car and then checked the identity of her visitor through the large picture window. It was a glorious day outside, blue skies, bright sun, it all boded well for the fun, eventful night she had planned.

"I'm ready. I'm going," Matt said as he rushed down the hall, duffle bag in hand.

"It's not like I'm trying to kick you out or anything, you know?" Erica chortled as she opened the door.

"I know." Matt smiled, kissing her briefly in farewell. "I want to go to the police station first, like I told you, before I head over to Nate's. Even though we're supposed to be hanging out and taking it easy for the day, if I'm late he's bound to rib me."

Erica chuckled. "If you are, then don't let him get away with it. You're doing important junior detective work, so you're allowed to be late."

"Exactly." Matt grinned before kissing her again. "Okay, I'm going. I love you, and I'll see you tomorrow morning," he said, hurrying over the threshold and down the stairs.

As he passed Seeley, who'd parked her car beside the garage and was just about to mount the stairs herself, they high-fived each other like a tag team.

"You're on guard duty now," he told her. "Keep my woman safe."

Erica's mouth shot open. "Excuse me," she yelled out to him.

"Will do, boss," Seeley called over her shoulder in agreement.

Although she'd secretly kind of liked the term, Erica moved her hands to her hips as she watched Matt throw the duffle bag into the back seat of his car before opening the driver's side door. Even from this distance, looking to where his car was parked on the other side of the driveway, Erica could see the affectionate wink he shot in her direction. It made her smile. Then, he was in the car, the engine roaring to life before the tires crunched on the gravel and he was heading back up the lane toward the street.

Seeley waved good-bye from the porch and then walked over to Erica, a heavy bag of her own in hand. "I didn't know Dr. Loverboy had moved in?"

Seeley's playful smirk was enough to have Erica scoffing in her own defense.

"No one's officially moved in with anyone. Matt just brought some of his things over after the little incident the other night. He'll be doing the same tomorrow until the police figure out who's behind it."

"Sure. Whatever you say."

Scowling at her friend, Erica grabbed Seeley's arm and yanked her inside, then closed the door behind them, locking it as usual now just in case.

"If you don't behave then I'll start asking you about Tom and whether or not you're defining yourselves as an *item*."

Seeley returned her glare, but a smirk pulled at her lips.

"If you did, then I might say yes, but as you haven't actually asked, I'm keeping my lips sealed."

"Oh my gosh. Really?"

Seeley just shrugged.

"Oh, come on, Seels, you have to tell me."

Seeley's gaze narrowed. "I'm here to help you tidy up and get things ready for the girls' night. I don't remember anything in that job description which includes chatting about my current relationship."

"Relationship? Wow, Seels, and he's not a hairy, tattooed biker. I'm so happy for you." Erica was virtually bouncing with glee, but then her eyes grew wide. "Can't you please tell me a little? I like Tom, and I want to know what he did to win you over."

Seeley searched her face, then sighed. "Fine. On our lunch break, but right now we've got work to do."

Erica clapped her hands together. "Yes, ma'am. Cleaning first, boy-talk later."

Seeley just rolled her eyes, a smile still tugging at the corners of her lips as she entered farther into the house.

"It's Tonya," Seeley told Erica after checking through the kitchen window. "Looks like she's got Yasmin and Vicky with her."

Erica glanced up from where she was organizing the food Nicolette, Hannah, and the twins, Chloe and Anabelle, had brought along. They were going to have chips and dips and carrot sticks coming out of their ears, but at least no one would go hungry.

Erica came to stand beside Seeley, peering out at their new arrivals, who were lit up almost as though in daylight from the bright glow of the porch lights. Like the other women already inside, Tonya and her friends had opted for clothing which rated higher in comfort level than style. With no men attending, there seemed little point in dressing up, especially when they were all planning to spend the evening lounging and eating anyway. Colorful tracksuits, some even velour, were the outfit of choice, while Erica, Seeley, and Nicolette had all settled on jeans and a comfortable shirt.

"Want me to go let them in?" Seeley asked her.

"Please." Erica nodded. "Show them to the living room, let them get comfortable and if they have any food stuffs they want sorted into bowls or whatever, just let me know."

Seeley looked over her shoulder to the crowded kitchen island countertop, where bowls, plates, and packets of all different snack foods had been arranged. "Do you even have enough bowls?"

"If I run out," Erica told her, "I can always use the colander, or I'm pretty sure there's some wide-brimmed hats in the closest."

Seeley laughed. "Now I understand why they call you creative."

Erica shoved her friend in the direction of the entry and then returned to her task of organizing the night's unhealthy buffet. As she heard Seeley greet the young women in a friendlier tone than usual, Erica wondered if she had Tom to thank for the pleasant change in Seeley's attitude. Apparently, he'd finally won her over with his taste in music, matching Seeley's love of country rock song for song, and because of his resilience, his determination to prove that his genuine affection for her was more than anything her beloved bad boys could offer.

The loud *crunch* of tires on the gravel driveway had Erica lifting her gaze from emptying yet another packet of chips into a bowl to glance out through the kitchen's picture window. The dark sedan that had just arrived sent chilled fingers clawing up her spine. Even though she recognized the car as Diana's and no longer believed, even though Matt remained unconvinced, that she was a potential suspect, seeing a near-identical car in almost exactly the same spot as it had been on that terrifying night had her breaking out in a cold, fearful sweat.

"Diana and Lauren are here," Seeley called out from the entry. "I'll let them in, then I'll lock up."

"Okay," Erica yelled out her answer as Tonya entered the kitchen.

"I've got some goodies for you, hon." She smiled before giving her a quick hug in greeting.

Erica wasn't quite sure how they'd got to the hugging stage of their friendship, but she wasn't about to argue over it with the girlfriend of her partner's best friend. She was just grateful that Tonya had found love elsewhere instead of wanting to fight for Matt's attention as she had in the beginning.

"The girls have brought crackers and dip and a packet of cookies," Tonya continued, "but I thought we all might need something a little more substantial."

Grinning, she pulled a box of party-pies and another of mini-sausage rolls out of the canvas bag in her hand and popped them on the edge of the countertop beside her. Erica hadn't had those treats since she was a child. It might not have been the healthier option, but at least it would help soak up some of the organic wine Lauren had offered to bring.

"Good thinking, Tonya. Do you want to help and stick them in the oven?"

The younger, bleached-blonde woman frowned at her. "Oh, hon, I'd love to, but I'm not domesticated. Ask me to pour a beer and I've got your back, but kitchen appliances—I'll be lucky if I don't burn down the place." Giggling, she patted Erica on the shoulder and then headed back out of the room.

Erica watched Tonya leave before hearing her melodious voice pipe up in the living room. Shaking her head, she picked up the box of party-pies and read the heating instructions on the back. She heard Seeley greet Lauren and Diana, heard their footsteps enter the house and the *thud* of the door, the *click* of the lock before noticing she once again had company in the kitchen. Glancing up, she saw Lauren making her way into the room, two heavy bags full of wine bottles in her hands.

"Evening, Lauren. Here, can I help you?" Erica reached the slender woman, grabbing a bag from her white-knuckled fingers before perching it on the cool glass stovetop and encouraging her to do the same.

"Thanks." Lauren smiled. "I wasn't sure how many to bring. I hope six is okay?"

"Six is heaps, thank you. I'd only hoped for two."

Lauren's cheeks blossomed pink with blush. As if only just noticing the massive number of snacks littering every smooth surface, her green eyes grew large. "Do you want a hand?"

"Oh God, yes." Erica sighed heavily. "Seeley was helping before everyone arrived, but I sent her off to watch the flock, so it's just been me for the past twenty minutes."

"What would you like me to do?"

"Well"—Erica looked around at the neat clutter of plates and bowls before turning back to the bags filled with wine—"if you don't mind pouring some glasses, we could get the drinks to the girls first and then start bringing out the food."

"Done," Lauren agreed as she began removing bottles from the carry bag.

As Erica did the same with the bag in front of her, she noticed something a little peculiar.

"These have been opened?" Erica held one closer to Lauren in an effort to show her the seal below the screw-cap had already been broken.

The hot pink tinge returned to Lauren's cheeks. "I hope you don't mind. I sometimes consider myself a bit of a connoisseur, so I like to check each bottle to make sure it's good." She took the wine from Erica and pointed at the label. "Did you know that two bottles of the same wine can taste totally different?"

"I'm pretty sure I've heard that somewhere, but I didn't think it could be true."

"Yes. It's usually due to batch variation, the fact that one type of wine can be housed in different casks or tanks, which can, in turn, change the consistency of the flavor." Lauren waved a hand in the air and then giggled. "It's just a little quirk of mine. It doesn't matter."

"Well, I've learnt something new tonight." Erica chuckled at her new friend's unusual habit, but was pleased to see Lauren speaking so avidly about something. "Good wine is *so* important. Maybe I'll have to start checking bottles in the future myself?"

"You've got to make sure you pick the very best for your guests," Lauren beamed. She turned her attention to the cabinets above the stove, pointing at them. "Now, where are your wine glasses?"

CHAPTER 29

It was still early, not even nine, and people were already getting sleepy. Nicolette had drifted off a little while ago, curled up on a spare duvet thrown over an air mattress. Yasmin and Anabelle were heading the same way too, with both now cuddled together, eyes closed on the end of the opposite sofa. Diana, who was sitting beside them, was squinting at the television, then rubbing her eyes as though she was desperate to stay awake. Even Hannah, a bookish brunette who had been singing along to the pop songs earlier in the romantic comedy, and Vicky, a petite redhead with a fondness for expletives, were also struggling to keep their eyes open as they watched the film from the comfort of another air mattress. Erica couldn't believe they were only halfway through their second movie and the girls were dozing off like babies during a car ride.

She yawned loudly, her own vision blurring just slightly, tiredly as she glanced around the disorderly room full of women, cozy blankets, and half-demolished food. It looked nothing like the pristine perfection she and Seeley had created when they'd organized the space. As her eyes roamed the area, Erica noticed Tonya and Chloe, who had made themselves comfy on the sofa beside her, had also succumbed to sleep. Giggling to herself at their lack of stamina, she caught Seeley's gaze across the room, from where she'd propped herself up in a comfortable pile of cushions. At least her best friend was wide-awake, but perhaps that was because she'd decided not to drink tonight. She had said before the night began that she'd wanted to stay alert and that meant keeping her wits about her without the tiring influence of alcohol. Erica had even seen her turn down Lauren's persuasive offer of wine, which for Seeley, probably meant that she was harnessing all of her willpower.

That had Erica trying to remember something—what was it? Alcohol? The wine. There was more of Lauren's wine, two bottles to be exact. She was too tired herself, so relaxed from the delightful beverage and the mountain of junk food she'd consumed throughout the romance movie-fest that she couldn't imagine having anything besides a cup of tea to try to keep herself awake. But, she was supposed to be playing hostess, and that meant keeping her guests happy, so she should at least ask them, shouldn't she?

Erica tried to stand but found herself a little wobbly. Lauren, who had taken a seat on the sofa beside her, quickly reached out to steady her.

"Are you okay?"

"Sure," Erica nodded, her eyes closing with the brisk movement. "Just going to get more wine."

"I don't think you need any more," Seeley commanded. "You're already pickled."

Erica shook her head, her eyes fluttering as she swayed backward toward the sofa cushions. Catching her balance with Lauren's help, she opened her eyes to stare at Seeley. "Not for me"—she gestured, encompassing the room—"but for the girls."

Seeley looked around, observing the lethargic forms littering the living room. Pushing herself to her feet, she came quickly to Erica's side and took her arm securely in hers. "Maybe it's time we put you to bed?"

"No," Erica protested, hearing the child-like shrill of her voice and immediately hating that she sounded so petulant. She shook her head. "Tea then. I'll make everyone some caffeinated tea. Maybe it will help to keep us awake."

She knew her words were slurring, that she was obviously under the influence, but it didn't make sense to her how she could've ended up so tipsy so fast. She'd only had three glasses of wine, one white, two red, over two and a half hours and had always had a high tolerance to alcohol. She couldn't understand what had gone wrong.

"Right," Seeley sounded reluctant. "Let's go make your guests some tea."

As she began to help Erica wobble away from the sofa and toward the entry, Lauren jumped up beside them, grabbing Erica's free arm.

"Let me," she said hastily. "It's probably my fault anyway." Her gaze dropped to the floor, her shoulders sagging. "I'm the one who brought the wine after all."

Seeley looked from Erica to Lauren and back again. "I'm not sure, Lauren. Erica can be a handful when she's drunk."

"I'm not drunk," Erica protested indignantly.

Seeley pursed her lips as though holding back a laugh.

"Really. I'm very happy to help." Lauren pleaded. "I feel responsible for how the night has played out. Let me at least help Erica make some tea to try to fix all this."

Seeley sighed, her bright blue eyes once again searching Erica's face. "Erica? Lauren's going to help you make the tea, okay?"

Erica frowned, finding it a little difficult to understand her friend through the ringing that had started in her ears. Her stomach was churning, making her feel nauseated.

"Erica, is that all right?" Seeley asked her again.

Erica's gaze drifted to Lauren's pleasant features, her kind smile, and she nodded at Seeley. "Sure, Lauren can help me make tea."

Erica grasped tightly onto Lauren's arm as Seeley released her supporting hold.

"Are you sure you don't need some help?"

Erica heard the worry in Seeley's tone as her friend once again checked in with Lauren.

"No," Lauren replied, shaking her head. "We'll be fine. It won't take us long."

As Lauren led her toward the brightly-lit entry, which connected to the kitchen, Erica leaned closer to her.

"You're always so nice," Erica said on a giggle. "So nice." She looked up at Lauren with wide eyes. "Do you like *herbal* tea? I've got lots of herbal teas."

*

Matt's yawn was louder than he'd expected when he stretched his arms to the ceiling, trying to work out the kinks which had formed after sitting, playing poker at Nate's for the last couple of hours. He was glad to have finally made it home to his basic little apartment after the long day. Actually, if he was honest with himself, it was the first day in a few days that he'd been home for more than just a spare change of clothes.

Ever since Erica had received that threatening letter, he'd taken to sleeping at hers, doing his best to protect her and keep her calm at nighttime. Although she'd regained some external bravado recently and liked to pretend that she was mostly over the experience of seeing a strange car lurking ominously in front of her house in the middle of the night, Matt knew she was still severely disturbed by it all. He could see it in her eyes, in the tenseness of her limbs. She was so jittery, so unsettled, and for a good reason; whoever was menacing her, stalking her, was still out there.

Earlier in the day, when he'd dropped off the list at the police station, he'd been relieved to hear that Detective

Senior Constable Walsh was feeling certain they'd successfully narrowed their suspects to a final few. While he wouldn't relinquish their names, he thanked Matt for the list, explaining it would add further validation to their case if the names they had matched those he'd come up with. Discovering that they were close to the culprit and knowing his and Nate's list might be able to assist them had really put Matt's mind at ease. He'd barely slept the night before, stressing over it, over who could be behind the sinister letter and what their motives or endgame might be. Ruminating over all of the possibilities had made his head ache. Even now, if he let it, it could consume him again. He needed answers, wanted to know who was behind it and how he could stop them.

Grabbing his duffle bag from the floor, Matt headed down the short hall toward his bedroom. He found himself smiling as he reflected over the good day Nate and he had spent together. They'd shared a few stories, played a few games on Nate's enormous television, and even opened up about their respective relationships.

The only time things had gotten a little too serious, a little too gloomy, was when Matt reminisced with his buddy about his feelings on the night Erica had awoken him with a scream. It still haunted him, the immediate fear of the unknown, of why she'd screamed like that, her beautiful voice so terrified. He'd told Nate all about the dread, the absolute soul-eating horror which had filled him at the thought that something might have happened to her, that she would be taken from him in an instant and he would lose her forever. Unexpectedly, Nate had understood. He'd seemed a changed man, maybe only slightly, but enough to realize that his feelings for Tonya were true enough that he, too, feared losing her from his life.

Matt's smile widened as he considered the fact that love looked good on Nate and that his buddy seemed all the better person, all the better man because of it. Turning into his room, Matt switched on the lights instinctively, gazing down as he lowered the duffle bag to rummage through it. After pulling a small toiletries case free, he tossed the larger bag toward the bed, glancing up to watch as it landed. It was in that moment, that brief instant, that he saw it, the *monstrosity,* and his blood turned to ice.

CHAPTER 30

Erica had propped herself up on a stool, holding her body upright with the help of the cool granite countertop of the kitchen island. Even though she was the one who had offered to go and make the tea, it was Lauren who was actually doing all of the making.

"Are you sure I can't help?"

Erica frowned, the slurring was getting worse. It was a wonder Lauren could even understand her. Maybe she should've taken Seeley's advice and gone to bed?

Lauren offered her a smile over her shoulder but shook her head. "I've got everything under control."

Mirroring Lauren's grin, Erica nodded, then had to close her eyes to stop the continued movement from making her feel even more nauseated. When her vision returned to the slightly misty view she was getting used to, she watched Lauren pour the hot water from the jug into a single teacup.

"Aren't you having some?" Erica asked, knowing her voice sounded painfully childlike.

Lauren shook her head again. "This is a special one. Just for you."

Erica's grin widened. *Just for her?* Lauren was so nice.

"What flavor did you choose?" Erica could hear the *tinkling* of the teaspoon against the porcelain of the cup. It sounded pretty, the echoing *ring* as it filled the fuzzy silence around her.

"Peppermint," Lauren told her, her lips spread wide, her teeth so pearly white as she turned around, cup in hand.

"Yum." Erica mumbled the word as she licked her lips. Peppermint was a strong flavor, but very delicious, and it should make her stomach feel better.

"Here you are, Erica." Lauren sounded distant as she seemed to serenade her.

Erica could see Lauren was passing the cup to her, but she couldn't quite get her body to move properly so she could take it from the other woman. She stared at Lauren's hands, losing herself in the vision as two became four, became six, then more. Erica closed her eyes as she swooned a little, feeling as though her whole body was spinning around and around. Maybe she might be safer if she were just lying on the flat, stable floor? Then warm hands grasped around hers, pushing a hot, smooth surface between them, holding them, holding her steady. Erica opened her eyes to see Lauren supporting her, keeping the cup safely within her grasp.

"Drink up," Lauren told her. "I'm sure this will make you feel better."

Erica nodded. Yes, tea always made her feel better. She could smell the peppermint now, so sharp and sweet, just the scent of it soothed her.

As she raised the cup to her lips, Lauren's hands fell from hers, until only her fingertip was poised on the porcelain bottom, ready to lift, to tip the hot liquid toward Erica's mouth. Erica closed her eyes again as she prepared herself to enjoy the delectably warm liquid. She would feel better soon, she knew it, and the world would stop spinning and spinning and …

Her whole body listed to the side, and before she could

regain her balance, she crumpled to the cold floor below, the teacup falling, smashing piercingly against the hard tiles.

"You idiot!"

Erica had considered the shrieked criticism funny, had believed it had come from her own head, her own mocking thoughts, until she'd gazed up, her head lolling painfully to the side, to see the fury on little blonde Lauren Perry's face.

*

"It's a freaking painting!" Matt knew he was yelling, and that he shouldn't be yelling into his mobile phone at Detective Senior Constable Walsh, but he couldn't help himself. "A freaking painting. There's a huge freaking painting on my bed, in my bedroom, in my apartment."

He could hear the garbled response on the other end of the line, knew it was only difficult for him to understand because of the rage and fear that was currently filling him, making the blood that was rushing through his body *whoosh* loudly in his ears. Already he could hear the police sirens approaching, knew it wouldn't take them long to arrive, but still, it didn't seem to be enough.

"Calm down, sir." Detective Walsh's words registered in Matt's mind momentarily. "Can you tell me what it's a painting of?"

Matt's mouth opened as he searched for how to appropriately explain it. How could he possibly describe such a hideous thing? For all its aesthetic beauty, all its perfect symmetry, bold colors, and the clearly excellent skill of its artist, how could he relay just how utterly horrific it was? Its mere existence had him wanting to destroy it, to tear it apart with his own bare hands. It was sickening. He felt as though its foulness clung to him just by being in the same room as it. It made him want to vomit; this disgusting thing so artistically radiant and yet so violating, so immoral.

"Dr. Garrick? Matt, are you still there?"

Matt could hear the sirens getting closer now, thought he'd even heard the sound of a car parking out the front of his apartment building.

"Dr. Garrick, what is it? I need to know what the painting is of."

"Me," Matt groaned, the word hurting him as he said it. "The painting, it's of me."

*

"You stupid slut," Lauren screeched at her. "Why couldn't you have just eaten the cake like you were supposed to? I made it sweet for you. I made it extra sweet. You wouldn't have noticed anything as you ate it, *only after*, then everything would've been right and today would never have had to happen."

Even though her body ached slightly from the fall to the floor, Erica gazed up at the slender woman with the cute, blonde pixie-cut, and tried not to laugh. She didn't know what was wrong with her. Evidently, she was very upset, but Erica, in her current woozy state, couldn't comprehend why.

Was Lauren mad because she'd found out Erica had thrown the cake away? Had she seen it in the bin behind Erica's shop? It was a pretty cake, sure. It had lots of apple pieces and raspberries with almond slithers on top, but Erica hadn't wanted to get sick like all those girls at the lingerie party, so she'd done as Tonya had suggested and binned it. Seeing Lauren so furious, her normally attractive features contorted with seething temper, had Erica feeling suddenly bad now that she'd done so.

"Fine," Lauren growled as she stalked around the top of the kitchen island and over to where Erica still lay on her side on the tiled floor. "You obviously want this to be difficult, don't you? You want it to be painful. Oh, Erica, I can give you painful."

Lauren's emerald eyes grew wide as she examined the room, then yanked the heavy wooden cutting board from the countertop and raised it above her head.

*

"Matt!"

Detective Walsh was still on the line, trying to get his attention as Matt opened his front door to the pounding fist of another policeman. With the phone still to his ear, he pointed six of them in the direction of his room, not wanting to get anywhere near the atrocity again. Flashing blue and red lights lit up the parking lot below, casting bright carnival-like colors over the street beyond. As he stepped outside, hoping the fresh night air might clear the nausea from his stomach, he noticed that the people in the neighboring apartments had come out to see what all the commotion was about. He could already hear their whispers beneath another distant siren, already knew that the town's gossip grapevine was gaining fodder so that come tomorrow there would be a new dramatic story for them to share.

"Matt? Talk to me." Detective Walsh's voice was stern but tinged with concern. "I'm on my way there now. Have the squad cars arrived?"

Finally listening, Matt nodded to himself. "Yes." He glanced over his shoulder at the constables milling around inside his home. "I've let them in."

"Good." He could hear the relief in the detective's tone. "Forensics will be there soon, also. There's no need to worry. Your list of suspects was extremely helpful. We have a car heading out now, prepared to take the person we believe is responsible into custody."

Matt released the tense breath he'd been holding. "Who is it?"

"Dr. Garrick," Detective Senior Constable Walsh

became formal again, "you know I can't tell you that."

"Just tell me something," Matt roared. "I need to know. Was it someone on my list?"

There was silence on the other end of the line for a long moment, and Matt wondered if the call had lost connection, but then the detective finally spoke.

"Yes, Matt. It was."

"Shit." Matt couldn't believe it. He'd been right. It had to be Diana.

Then a cold, icy rush swept down his entire body as he realized that the police wouldn't be able to find her at her house, because she was still at …

"Erica's! She's at Erica's. You have to help Erica!"

*

It all seemed to happen in slow motion. The raised cutting board above Lauren's head, then it swooping down as she lowered it swiftly toward Erica's skull. Erica knew she should move, she should just roll away, but the cold floor had a hold of her, it was keeping her steady, and if she tried, she might fall, fall and keep falling.

Deep inside, she knew if the board connected, if Lauren hit her with it, kept hitting her, it wouldn't be good, but knowing that just wasn't enough to fight through the haze that had so completely consumed her. Instead, she did the only thing her body would allow her to—she closed her eyes.

As a hot tear trickled down Erica's cheek to the floor, she heard Lauren snarl.

"You should have stayed away from him like I told you to."

Then there was a yell, it sounded like Seeley, and something heavy clattered against the floor. Erica stretched her tired eyes open, trying to see the commotion, to understand why the pain she'd expected hadn't come. Seeley had tackled Lauren to the floor beside her and was sitting on top of her, fighting off her thrashing arms.

"No," Lauren was shrieking. "Get off me. No! She can't have him."

Erica watched as Lauren stretched a clawed hand out toward her, violently trying to reach her but to no avail. Instinctively, Erica tried to do the same, her fingertips crawling ever so slightly toward her, before Seeley wrestled Lauren's arm back and fought to hold her down.

"Don't even try it, you crazy bitch," Seeley growled.

Then Erica's aching eyes were closing and she drifted, rocking in a pitch-black sea which seemed to be swirling around and around and around, with only the wail of a distant siren keeping her from falling deeper into the bottomless abyss.

CHAPTER 31

A soft intermittent *beep* sound filled the darkness, growing louder with each second as though it were dragging Erica up from the depths of the black hole she'd lost herself in. Wearily, her eyelids fluttered open, revealing a clinically clean, white room and a familiar person gazing over at her.

"How are you feeling, Sleeping Beauty?" The whites of Seeley's lovely blue eyes were bloodshot, and dusky circles sat beneath them.

Erica's whole body seemed heavy as she shifted her position in the conventional white sheets of the hospital bed in an effort to sit up. The right side of her body ached as she did so, and there was a brief, sharp pain on the back of her left hand. Looking down at it, she noticed she was hooked up to an intravenous drip. As she glanced fuzzily around the small private room, her eyes burning from the bright fluorescent lighting, she tried to swallow the thick, dry lump at the back of her throat.

"Matt's just left to get us some coffee," Seeley continued, pulling Erica's gaze back to her. "He's been here the whole time, by your side, waiting for you to wake up."

Erica stared at her, her mind a bit jumbled, a little hazy. How had she ended up here? The last thing she remembered was being at home in the kitchen, making tea with Lauren. She rubbed at her tired eyes and then opened her mouth to speak.

"What time is it?" It was a croaky noise, barely audible.

"It's a little after two in the afternoon on Sunday." Seeley paused. "Do you remember much of Saturday night? The doctor said you might be a bit confused to begin with."

Erica frowned and rubbed at her eyes again as she struggled to remember.

She had been in the kitchen with Lauren. She'd been feeling so tired, had thought it might have been best for her to go to bed. Then, she remembered falling, the teacup shattering and … the fury on Lauren's face. It suddenly made sense why one side of her body ached as though it were bruised. She had hurt herself when she'd fallen from the stool to the hard, tiled floor.

Abruptly, another burst of memory hit her. A flash of Lauren's manic expression as she held the heavy, wooden cutting board over her head, above Erica's head. Memories flooded back until all the pieces clicked together.

Erica nodded at Seeley. "Lauren?" Her voice was so dry and raspy.

She wanted to ask what had happened to her, wanted to be sure she couldn't try to hurt her or anyone else again.

Seeley reached for the glass of water on the benchtop beside the bed and handed it to her. Erica took it gratefully and drank long and deeply, relishing the cool liquid on her arid throat.

"The police have her," Seeley explained. "They believe she spiked the wine with a combination of sedatives and painkillers. Apparently, she had prescriptions for all of them. It was just lucky I'd chosen not to drink. I'd considered it odd at the time that Lauren had been so persistent when offering me one, especially when she had barely touched her own glass. It was over the top, you know. She'd even left a glass of wine beside me, but I'd ignored it."

Erica swallowed another sip of water then put the glass back on the benchtop, before reaching for Seeley. "Thank you," she told her, her voice still hoarse. "I don't think I'd be here if it weren't for you."

She felt Seeley squeeze her hand and watched as her friend's expression hardened.

"There's more you should know." Seeley raked her other hand down the side of her face. "The police also tested the tea on the floor of your kitchen and the cake they found in the trash at Unique Art Boutique. Matt and I told them about it. We thought it might be of interest. Both contained a large quantity of rat poison."

Erica swallowed deeply, feeling suddenly queasy now. If Tonya hadn't told her to dispose of the cake, if she, herself, hadn't accidentally spilled that tea, what would have happened to her? Would she have been poisoned, horribly, painfully? Her stomach cramped at the possibility.

"Detective Senior Constable Walsh believes Lauren was behind the harassing calls you were receiving, that she was using an unregistered phone. When the police searched her apartment, they discovered a spare key to Diana's car, stolen apparently and ..." Seeley trailed off, her eyes examining Erica's, and then she released a lengthy sigh.

"They found a sort of shrine there, to Matt. It had some of his things. A copy of the key to his apartment, some clothes, underwear, lots of photos, even a toothbrush. But the most interesting thing was a speed-dating card from a few weeks ago, you know, the ones which list the names of the people you're about to meet and you can write whether you're interested or not interested? They use them to create matches and pass on contact details. Matt's name was on the list. The police suspect Lauren must have met him there and quickly developed a dangerous obsession for him. They think the gifts she'd arranged for him were a way to convince him of her love. But then you came on the scene and her motive changed, focusing not only on how to win him over, but on how to get rid of you."

Seeley slumped her shoulders as she wiped the back of her free hand over her sunken eyes. "I know it's a lot to take in. I don't quite fully understand it all myself. I guess I'm just so relieved I was able to do something, to stop her." She squeezed Erica's hand in hers again. "What kind of bestie would I be if I didn't have your back?"

Erica smiled at her. "You're not only my bestie, Seels, you're my family—and you have a mighty decent right-hook."

"You saw that?"

Erica nodded before glancing around the room. "Where are the others?"

"Oh, they're fine." Seeley gestured toward the closed door. "Most of the girls are in a couple of multi-patient rooms down the hall, but Tonya is in the room next door. When her father found out about it all, what I had done, he organized private rooms for you both. I think he's very grateful nothing happened to his precious angel." She chuckled lightly and then her eyes widened. "I forgot, I have big news to tell you."

"What?" Erica sat a little straighter in the bed.

"So, the world must be about to end, because … Nate hugged me and we're *friends* now, apparently." She used her fingers to make air-quotes around the suspect word. "He's so grateful I was there, that I kept you and Tonya safe. Of course, I'll always think he's an ass, but I guess he's growing on me."

"Wow. That's incredible, Seels."

Erica definitely hadn't expected that. Nate and Seeley, two people who had hated each other for the majority of their lives, were … *friends* now? Who would've thought?

Seeley smirked at her. "I'm so glad you're pleased about

it, because we're *all* having dinner with Jocelyn and Hamish next Saturday. Won't that be fun?" Sarcasm weighed heavily in her tone.

Erica's eyes widened. *Fun* wasn't exactly the word she'd use.

The *click* of the door handle had both women glancing up. As he entered, two Styrofoam coffee cups in hand, Matt's gaze instantly connected with Erica's. Her heart caught in her throat as she watched his expression light up at seeing her. She reached out to him instinctively, her eyes welling with tears as he rushed over to the bed.

"You're finally awake." His tired voice was choked with emotion.

Erica couldn't stop the tears from trailing down her cheeks as her chest constricted with the need to sob. She had so much she wanted to say to him, so much she needed to make sure he knew. She wanted to tell him again how much she loved him, how much she needed him in her life, but the words were trapped, her chest tight with them as though they were trying to struggle free of her precious heart itself.

"I'll give you two some time," Seeley told them as she stood, snatched her coffee from Matt, and headed for the door.

Erica wanted to acknowledge her friend's departure, wanted to thank her again, but she couldn't drag her attention away from Matt, couldn't find the right words.

As the door clicked closed, Matt grasped her hands in his, and he bent to kiss her lightly on the forehead and then the mouth.

"I love you, Erica." His voice was husky with affection. "Please don't ever scare me like that again. I couldn't bear to lose you."

Erica fought back another sob. "I love you, too," she told him, her voice strangled as hot tears continued to slide down her face.

As he kissed her again, she realized all her previous

fears of intimacy seemed insignificant now. She loved Matt and was no longer afraid to tell the whole world how she felt. She needed to be with him, to share her life with him, and to love him, just as he loved her. She could see that now, could understand how unique he was, how special their relationship could be, and that no matter what; he'd always be there for her, because his love, unlike all those before him, was wholeheartedly genuine.

*

"These can't all be for me?"

The wonder in Erica's voice as she looked at all the bundles of vibrant flowers filling her porch had Matt laughing.

Since it had been necessary for Lauren to receive treatment for the injuries she'd sustained during her scuffle with Seeley before being remanded in custody, the local police had organized strict security at the Maleny Memorial Hospital for all the women involved. Unfortunately, that had made it difficult for those in town to bring their support directly to the hospital room, so they had chosen to drop off their get-well-soon gifts at Erica's house and the homes of the others involved, instead.

"We care for each other here in Montville." He grinned. "It's a *small* town, don't you know?"

"Not from the number of flowers, it isn't." Erica gaped. "Every person must have dropped something off."

Well, not everyone, Matt thought.

He guessed Lauren was no longer considered to be a bona fide member of the township now that she was going to be spending some time behind bars.

A couple of nights ago, when he'd announced to Detective Senior Constable Walsh that his number one suspect, Diana, was in fact at Erica's, he'd quickly discovered that the detective had another person in mind. According to them, they believed it was Lauren who'd been behind the secretive presents he'd received, which had culminated in the hideous portrait of himself that he'd found on top of his bed. Besides being number five on his and Nate's suspect list for her association with Diana, the system at the police department had finally matched a third set of partial fingerprints on the keychain to an earlier record Lauren had had for attempted breaking and entering as a teenager. She'd also had a restraining order against her from an old boyfriend, which had been dropped when he'd moved overseas. Detective Walsh had explained that, with a record like hers, it was likely Matt was just the last in a line of men she'd taken a fanatical interest in, and that it was exceptionally lucky things had ended the way they had.

"Do I really deserve all of these?" Erica chuckled. It was a sweetly infectious sound. "I don't know where to put them all."

Matt gazed at her gorgeous face. Even shadowed by the slight purplish bruise on the side of her head from where she'd hit it on the tiled floor, he still considered her smile luminous.

She had been released from the hospital only that morning. Like all of the women who had been at Erica's that night, she'd been required to stay for observation in case she'd suffered adverse effects of the drugs Lauren had dispersed into the wine.

Matt dreaded to think about what might have happened had Seeley not been sober. His gut tightened in anger, in fear. He'd almost lost Erica, almost lost the woman he loved at the hands of some hysterical lunatic, and that had terrified him, it still haunted him. The chilling *what-ifs* made him eternally grateful for every moment, for every future second he got to spend with her.

"Of course, you deserve it," he told her. "I've no doubt the other women involved are receiving a home-coming similar to yours. The whole town was in shock after the incident, and we're relieved that you all made it through the night alive. Some of us *much* more than others."

Matt bowed his head as painful terror gripped his heart once more, but when he gazed back up at her, looking deeply into those big brown eyes, the tightness in his chest lessened, and he found himself smiling again. As Erica grinned back at him, he could see the love shining there, lighting up her face. She curled an arm around him, pulling him against her side as he cuddled closer, his palm smoothing over the coarse denim of her jean shorts.

When she flinched at his touch and moved his hand higher to her waist and the soft cotton of her black blouse, he remembered the other injuries she'd suffered in her fall. Her knee, hip, and shoulder were all purplish-black with bruising, but at least that would pass and she would heal. At least those injures weren't permanent like the alternative that Lauren had had in mind.

"Sorry," he said, kissing her uninjured cheek lightly before gesturing to the house as they climbed the steps to the porch. "Seeley and I, we cleaned it all up. She showed me where everything went, so it should look like before …" He paused, not wanting to say those words out loud. *Before you were attacked by a madwoman in your own home.* He didn't want to remind her. "I mean, it should look the way you like it."

As they reached the porch and the maze of colorful floral arrangements, Erica grinned over at him.

"Thank you. I owe you both so much. I don't know how I could possibly make it up to you."

"Well, Seeley's set," he chuckled as he remembered what Seeley had told him in the hospital. "Tonya's father has declared she can drink and eat free for life at the Montville Tavern. He's claiming he's doing it on your behalf, that you're a treasure to the town and Seeley's heroism shouldn't go unrewarded, but I think he was just overwhelmingly relieved his beloved daughter made it through the whole incident pretty much unscathed." Gently, he squeezed Erica a little closer to him. "As for me, being with you is gift enough."

"Really?" She cocked a dark eyebrow as she gazed up into his eyes.

Matt nodded and slipped his free arm gently around the other side of her waist, holding her body softly against him. "Really," he told her.

Erica lifted her head to briefly kiss his lips, like the light fluttering of butterfly wings, before pulling back to stare at him. She gave him that hypnotizing smile, that sultry grin which had had his heart melting and his groin throbbing with desire from the moment he first met her.

"I guess you don't want to move in with me then?"

Matt was stunned. If his jaw hadn't already hit the floor, it felt as though it was heading that way. "What?" The word came out in a burst.

Erica shrugged and pulled out of his arms, heading for her front door. "I mean, I just thought you might want to, because you say you love me and everything."

She had already released the deadlock and slipped the key into the door, before his wits returned to him.

Had she really just asked him that? Did she actually want him to move into her home, into her space? Was she really wanting to share her life with him?

Matt wanted to jump for joy, wanted to soar, it was as though her words had given him wings. For Erica, moving in with a loving partner was an enormous step, but if she was ready for that, then one day soon she could be ready for more, maybe even the big question—maybe even … *marriage*.

As he hurried over to her, she pushed in the front door.

"Oh well, maybe I was wrong? Maybe you don't love me, maybe you don't want to move in with me?" There was humor in her tone as she kept her back to him and stepped over the threshold.

Excitement and utter delight buzzed through Matt like electricity. It was all he could do not to yell his answer, his desire to the entire universe.

"Marry me!" He'd blurted out the words before he'd had time to think them through. Dashing in front of her, he clasped her hands in his, the biggest, most exuberant grin spreading his lips as he dropped down to one knee. "Marry me, Erica. I love you. You know I love you, and I know you love me, too. Take a chance on me, Erica. Trust me. Marry me."

She was everything he'd ever wanted, it all hinged on this, her answer, that one little word which could change his life forever.

Erica stared at him, her beautiful coffee brown eyes wide, before the corners of her rosy lips curled upward. "You're crazy," it was barely a whisper, "but I do trust you, Matt, and I love you, too, with all of my heart."

Then she nodded, a confident, decisive nod, and Matt knew it, he just knew she was his.

"Yes, Matt," Erica beamed. "Of course, I'll marry you."

The End.

CHECK OUT THESE BOOKS BY TAMMY MANNERSLY

You can't hide from destiny....

Callum Hawthorne is one of those lucky guys who seem to have it all. He's a wealthy property tycoon, the CEO of his family's company. He's handsome, intelligent and charming and has a gorgeous new woman on his arm every week. But there's one thing still missing – the love of his life, Lucy Spencer.

Fourteen long years ago, Lucy left for college and cut off all contact with Cal, leaving their mutual friend Madison as his only connection. That was until in his effort to save his deceased father's beloved Gold Coast property, The Calypso, Cal contacts Insight Marketing, the best advertising firm in Melbourne, and discovers his Lucy among the team.

Successful marketing executive, Lucy Spencer had managed to avoid her ex-best friend for nearly half their lives. Fearful of trusting him, loving him and having her heart broken all over again, Lucy tries to keep her distance from him, but discovers that there is a fine line between love and hate, and maybe – just maybe – Cal could be her inescapable destiny.

~Persuading Lucy was a 1st Place WINNER for the prestigious Chatelaine Book Awards for Romance Fiction and will quickly become your new favourite read.

Invited by one brother, tempted by the other…

Former Australian playboy Blake Davenport knows his billionaire brother, David, is capable of anything to ensure he gets what he wants. But manipulating his young daughter's beautiful teacher into marriage is unacceptable.

Gwen Deveraux is grateful for the invitation to spend Christmas and New Year's with her beloved student's family, especially when her handsome host is so eager for her company. After surviving a broken heart, she is finally ready to give love another chance.

But, who with?

The illustrious David Davenport whose real motives seem hidden behind charm? Or his roguish brother, Blake, who has tempted her heart and body from the very moment they met?

NOW AVAILABLE IN EBOOK AND PRINT AT ALL MAJOR BOOK RETAILERS.

TAMMY MANNERSLY

ABOUT THE AUTHOR

Tammy Mannersly is an Australian author based in Brisbane, Queensland. She loves writing romance, has a fondness for animals, is crazy about movies and enjoys a great Happily Ever After. Her passion for writing started from a very young age and led her to complete a Bachelor Degree in Creative Industries majoring in Creative Writing at Queensland University of Technology. Her novel, *Persuading Lucy*, was a 1st Place WINNER in the 2018 Chatelaine Books Awards for Romantic Fiction, a Chanticleer International Book Awards competition.

You can find out more information about Tammy and her work on her website: www.tammymannersly.com or by visiting:

Facebook:
https://www.facebook.com/tammymannersly

Goodreads:
https://www.goodreads.com/author/show/16935790.Tammy_Mannersly

Instagram:
https://www.instagram.com/tammymannersly/

Twitter: https://twitter.com/TammyMannersly